DARK EDGE PRESS

THIS
PLACE OF
HAPPINESS

NICKI HERRING

Published in 2022 by Dark Edge Press.

Y Bwthyn
Caerleon Road,
Newport,
Wales.

www.darkedgepress.co.uk

Text copyright © 2022 Nicki Herring

Cover Design: Jamie Curtis

Cover Photography: Canva

A CIP catalogue record for this book is available from the British Library.

ISBN (eBook): B09XYTZ52D
ISBN (Paperback): 979-8-8217-5877-4

CONTENTS

Dedicated to the boys: my husband, Steve Herring; my son, Sam Herring; and my dad, David Ridout.

I give you the four directions of the world, as we do not know where you will be at the end of your life.
A Tuareg Blessing

CHAPTER ONE

Amti Nassima wants me to stop and listen. But I won't. No doubt an aunt is pregnant again or the butcher is taking a third wife. Or Grandmother has found another reason to be angry with me because of something I haven't done; but even *I* can't have screwed up when I've been working at the hotel for the last ten hours. All I want to do is lie on my bed and read a book with my feet up against the wall.

When I first came to live with this family, my family, in their rotting Ottoman palace in the Casbah, high above the old French quarter of Algiers, I imagined a life as a princess in *The Arabian Nights*; but now I am more like a girl from the slave market who's been sold by Barbary pirates to an evil djinn: my grandmother, Mani Aïcha. She wasn't always like this towards me. I was her favourite when Dad was here, but after he left, she changed. As if she can't bear to look at me. One look at my face blows her smiles away.

She's back. Sitting in the courtyard by the fountain.

It's been odd. She's been going out all day since last Wednesday, and Gossip HQ has gone into overdrive. They stop talking every time I walk past the door. And start talking about the weather. As if this was England. And they aren't good at it. In England we have so many words for mist or drizzle or peeing cats and dogs, but their meteorological vocabulary isn't so extensive. The aunties and older cousins sit round the table, hands idle, watching me clearing up and washing up after every meal. When Grandmother is here, they don't get to sit still either.

There have always been different levels of rumours and gossip in the kitchen. There is 'married woman' gossip. I assume they are talking about sex because they gasp and giggle over it, and won't share because heaven forbid I learn anything before 'the sex chat' when I get married. Except I don't have a mum for that. Maybe Amti Nassima will do it. She'll make it funny. Please God, not Grandmother or it will be 'lie back and think of Algeria' for the rest of my life.

Then there is 'mother gossip'. Proud mothers discussing the aptitude displayed by their toddlers. And how to toilet-train them. I'm sure I'll find it interesting one day . . . But something is going on this evening. The house is full. Everyone is here. Something is up. And everybody seems to know about it except me.

They don't mean to be unkind. It isn't that they don't care. They are busy, and why would I need mothering when I have so much of Grandmother's attention, even if it is negative? And there are so many uncles and aunties and husbands and wives. My cousins and all the other children fill every room. After two years I still don't know all their names and I have never found time to count them, but they are here from sunrise to sunset. They never stop chattering and wanting. 'Rabia, Rabia, Rabia!' The sound of my own name makes me want to hide in a cupboard without a handle. Call to prayer isn't for another two hours, but until then it will be, 'Rabia, Rabia, Rabia, take off your veil. Put on a smile. Place the bowls gently on the table, Rabia. Don't drop them, Rabia.'

It's better at the hotel. I started as a waitress, but after I found the sewing room I couldn't stay away. All the sewing goes through that room. Everything. A tablecloth that needs a hem mending. A tea towel with enough life in it to warrant some darning. The king-size sheets that have enough fabric in them to be cut down for a single bed. And there are no machines. Everything is sewn by hand. Exquisite little stitches sewn under bright daylight lamps. I started learning from the girl doing alterations for the boutique. When they realised I'm fast and neat they let me go there regularly. Staying late after work. Doing little bits. When they saw I had a fine touch on silk the girl from the boutique, Leila, let me hem the wedding dresses, and when she got married there was a job for me. It wasn't a promotion. I earn exactly the same as a waitress, but I am learning to sew with silver threads and to make lace. My boss tells her customers that she has a seamstress from England, as if I'm special. Her only complaint is the state of my hands so I'm not allowed to meet the customers; but I can hardly tell Grandmother that I need some dinar to buy washing-up gloves and hand cream. I can hear it now, 'I never had creams, Rabia, and my hands haven't fallen off.'

If I were granted three wishes by Grandmother Djinn, I would study textile design in Paris. Or even embroidery at the Royal School of Needlework at Hampton Court. Ali and I would, by some miracle, manage to fall in love with each other . . . and Dad would come back.

But I'm not here to daydream. It's Gathering Day today. Friday. Every Friday the family swarms around Grandmother like ants on a jam sandwich. They keep coming despite the over-seasoned stews and never-ending couscous. The seven casseroles bubble on the low heat until after evening prayers and their steam fills the small square kitchen. Flat breads are stacked in the oven and the ingredients for omelettes are arranged on the table next to the hob. I need more bowls today, and there aren't enough. In one corner of the kitchen a dirty grey curtain made from a haik, a traditional long veil, hides a jumble of unwashed dishes and saucepans. The pans are sticky with grease and dust, and I hold them at arm's length on the way to the sink, run the cold water and add a handful of grated soap. I put the kettle on. There's never enough hot water on Fridays. I wrap an apron over my skirt and sigh. The carbolic soap stings my hands but, if I don't wash up, no one else will. There are dishes to put on the table. Then more cooking. More cleaning and tidying up. None of the aunts has been working since six this morning as I have, but they sit chatting while Amti Nassima makes pretty patterns with almonds and sliced grapes on the desserts. I love desserts. We only get desserts on Gathering Day.

Leaving the dishes to dry on a tray next to the sink, I grab two large jugs of orange squash and a stack of bright plastic beakers. The children will be getting thirsty. I leave Nassima to her fiddling.

Grandmother is sitting on the ledge of the fountain with Dahkman, my dad's brother, kneeling beside her. When I was a little girl Dahkman and my dad fixed the fountain and it ran for the whole summer, but when we came back a year later it had stopped. They didn't try again. That first summer was different. The fountain running into the glassy pool took the heat out of the day, and Dad's joy at being home took the sting out of Grandmother. If Ali were the plumber's son instead of the baker' it would be worth marrying him just to have the fountain mended and the problems with the hot water sorted out.

I keep to the shadows under the arched columns, hoping to get to the table without Grandmother seeing me. This route under the balconies is longer, but the dusty tiles soothe my tired feet and after putting the jugs on the table I return to the shade. My feet don't make a sound as I walk close to the wall. I picture myself as the little nun in my favourite romance, before she's rescued from the convent by the man she can't refuse. I don't look up. It is quicker if I don't make eye contact with Grandmother.

Back in the kitchen Nassima passes me the silver tray and the blue teapot that belonged to Grandmother's heroic father, which only comes out on special occasions. She's arranged three of the gold-edged tea glasses around it. I take one off. I have to go to Grandmother with her tea, but I really don't want to sit and listen while they try to persuade me again to marry Ali. I might be desperate but, much as I love him, even *I* have limits. Concentrating on the tray balanced on my left palm, I walk to the centre of the courtyard and get into position to pour the tea. After a million scolding's I have learnt to pour the tea like a Tuareg. But nothing is good enough for Grandmother.

'Hold the tray higher,' she says. 'Stop rattling the glasses. This isn't afternoon tea at your hotel.'

The arching stream froths into the little glasses. I place the tray on the table and hand Grandmother and Dahkman their drinks, at which point the teapot wobbles, slopping tea onto the tray.

Grandmother sighs, 'I asked for three glasses. Get me another glass.'

'I don't want any tea–'

'Why would the tea be for you? You aren't a princess, to be sitting and drinking tea when we've a family to feed.'

And that's when I see the girl next to Grandmother. I rush off to retrieve the extra glass, pushing past the two aunties stood gossiping with Nassima in the kitchen doorway.

After pouring the third cup of tea I place the glass on the palm of my right hand, extending the handle to the guest.

'Thank you,' she says. In English. Proper English, spoken with an English accent.

I get a better look at her and am shocked at how much like me she looks. Not the family resemblance of cousins, not similar-shaped eyes – exactly like me. My face. My hair, just like I used to wear it before Grandmother took the hairbrush and tore through all my tangles until it was tamed and pulled back to sit tidily under a scarf. I know she wishes I had been as easy to subdue. I compare my hands, the shape of my nails, with hers. My knuckles are red and sore-looking. Her hands are soft, manicured and tidy. She sniffs the tea before she sips. At the bottom of her jeans, her feet are bare.

'Thank you,' she says again.

I don't reply. Is she the reason for all the gossip? Nassima has to tell me now.

Back in the kitchen I find Nassima waiting for me.

'Who is that girl?'

'That's what I was trying to tell you. You wouldn't wait.'

Nassima pushes the saucepan to the back of the hob and lowers the gas. She wipes her hands on a tea towel, takes off Grandmother's short wide apron and takes me by the hand. 'Come with me.' She leads me back through the doorway into the courtyard.

Grandmother is now holding the girl's hands and my uncle has moved to sit with them on the low wall, so the girl is sandwiched between them. When he sees us coming, he leans towards Grandmother and whispers. Grandmother nods and lets go of the girl's hands.

Dahkman stands and says, 'Rabia, this is Amal. She is your sister . . . Mokhi's other daughter.'

'What other daughter?' I turn to Nassima, but she is smiling at the girl. I don't know if I should shake her hand, this Amal, or step forward to hug her with two kisses, or slap her. Why is she here? Will she be trapped, like me? Nassima breaks the silence by gathering the empty glasses onto the tray. Should I wait, or help, or run off and hide in my bedroom? Grandmother's lips are a little thinner, and her eyes a little narrower, but she takes the girl's hands again and ignores me for now.

Nassima picks up the tray and pushes her hip against mine. I find myself moving back to the kitchen, propelled into motion like an automaton that just needed to be prodded in the right direction. Nassima leads me back to the kitchen and passes me two more jugs of juice. 'Be nice to her, Rabia.'

'Why should I be nice? Someone should have warned me. Everyone knew about her except me, didn't they?'

Nassima won't look at me.

'You knew, didn't you, Nassima?'

'Only recently. No one knew anything about her until a fortnight ago, when Grandmother got a letter. She only wants to meet your dad.'

'She'll be lucky.'

'Rabia . . . be nice.'

I bring the jugs back to the table, and as I walk past the girl, I flick my foot against her ankle. The soles of her feet are showing. She doesn't get it, just carries on watching me, so I flick her foot again on the way back, and this time she reacts.

'Ow.'

Grandmother grabs my skirt, bunching its hem as she drags me closer to pinch my leg, her blunt nails bruising me through the cotton. I refuse to give

Grandmother the pleasure of my tears. Instead, I glare at the girl, frozen by the pain of the pinch. I should be welcoming her, saying nice things, but my confusion pours out instead. 'My dad told me I should never say sorry, because I should never do anything I am sorry for. But he was a shit to us. Leaving without saying goodbye.'

I want to keep going, to tell her that if she is looking for Dad, she will be disappointed in so many ways. Disappointed by his absence and just as disappointed by the man she finds. If she finds him. But I am interrupted by my uncle Dahkman, who rises and straightens with the elegance of a man who prays on his knees, head touching the ground, five times a day. I have never seen him so angry.

'Rabia! If my brother, may Allah be kind to him, never explained . . .' He pauses, rethinks, his finger and thumb held together while he considers. Shaking his head, he says, 'Apologise to your older sister or leave.'

I'm going to miss the best meal of the week. The fresh pastries and Nassima's trifles. I won't show them that I care. That this matters. I tighten my scarf over my hair and grab my bag. I am not going to apologise to my know-nothing sister. I don't know why it's rude to show the soles of our feet either, but it is.

I walk to the bottom of the stairs that rise in a spiral round the courtyard. Ten steps up, and I'm on the first balcony. They are all watching. I walk to the corner. Five more steps and turn onto the next balcony. Two little cousins have come out of their rooms and watch as I walk past. I desperately search for something clever to say to explain my behaviour. I want my sister to understand that I am . . . I don't know what I am. Sorry? Defeated? A sister worth loving? Five more steps. Another balcony. They are still watching me, like a family of meerkats, turning as I turn. I reach the spiked wooden main door with its shuttered grill. I pull Grandmother's haik off its peg, tearing it in the process. Another sin, but the one thing I can do perfectly is sew and mend. She'll never know. I pause at the door and look down. Dad had another daughter. He never mentioned this other girl. Now I am only the second daughter and the second best. It is my jealousy that rises into words, and I shout down from the balconies, making sure that she hears every word. 'He wasn't your dad. Just your father. And can someone teach her some manners? We don't show the soles of our feet, Amal. Not here.'

Dahkman stares up at me. 'Then who better than you to teach her about him, Rabia? To teach her all the little things she doesn't know.'

I turn away, push on the heavy door and, once on the other side, slam it back in place with both hands. I have nowhere to go. I could walk down to the harbour. It isn't far, but young women don't walk past the cafés on their own on a Friday evening. I cover myself in the long white haik that reaches to the ground. A haik should reach just above your ankles but Grandmother is short and wide and her haik swamps me. That's why I took it. My own portable hiding place. Wrapping myself in the cotton folds, I stop at the steps cut in the wall further up the alleyway. I sit here, my face covered so that no one will see me crying. I know that everything has changed, sudden as a rainstorm in an

English summer. Will she be trapped here like me? If she likes me, she might help me to leave . . . but why should she help me when I've kicked her twice and had a tantrum?

The shadows move higher up the walls as the sun lowers in the sky. When the muezzin start their call to prayer I climb the steps to hide in an archway. The wall is cool against my back. The men pass on their way to the mosque and when they're gone, I go back to my steps and wipe my eyes, but too soon. Someone else is coming. I pull the haik lower, but they stop. Worn work boots at the bottom of a pair of floury trousers. Ali. My friend. I push the haik back from my face and look up. He puts his hands in front of his stomach, pretending to hold a bag, mimicking Grandmother, and bends his knees to lean down.

'What have you done wrong today?' But I don't smile. He wipes a tear from my face with the side of his thumb and sits beside me. His leg against mine. I lean my head on his shoulder and breathe the scent of yeast and fresh bread.

'I heard,' he says.

'Heard what?'

'You've got a visitor.'

'Does everybody in the Casbah know, except me?'

'I expect so. Do you want to talk about her?'

'No.' I lean away from him, against the wall. Ali follows and leans against me. I push back at him, trying to make him sit straight.

'Don't sit so close. They'll have us married by teatime.' Ali has an enormous smile full of crooked teeth. He puts an arm round my shoulder and leans down to kiss the top of my head.

'Is this all I need to do?' he says.

I shove him away. 'You don't want to marry me. And my dress isn't finished. My dress is going to take years.'

'So it's only the dress you're worried about? Think about it, Rabia. If we get married, we can leave here. We can go to England and get divorced.'

'You need to work on your marriage proposals, Ali.'

I don't remember a time when I didn't know Ali. We both lived in London when we were kids, and when we came here, in the school holidays visiting our families, it was a relief to speak English. To talk to someone who understood what it was to be not quite English in England, but a foreigner when we came 'home' to Algeria. It would be easy to say yes to him and Grandmother. But I don't love him. Not like that. And he doesn't love me. I want to fall in love with a man who makes my heart melt and my knees wobble. And Ali wants a man like that too.

He takes my hand and looks at my sore knuckles. 'One day, little Rabia, we are going to meet our heart's delight, and we'll be happy. You'll have time to read and sew and cook truly horrible dinners just like your gran.'

'And you'll go back to England and sell the best pastries north of Algiers.'

'That's why you should marry me. I'll keep you from starving. And your grandmother would get cheap bread.' He pulls me to my feet.

'Will they notice you didn't get to Mosque?'

'I'll tell them I was with you.'

I stand on tiptoes to kiss his cheek. 'No, you won't.'

He slaps the dust from the seat of his trousers and a fine haze of flour settles on his shoes. He watches to make sure I get back into the house safely.

The door won't open quietly. I doubt it ever did. The bell at the top of the door in a village shop is quieter, but if you open it just enough to squeeze through it doesn't make so much noise. The house is quiet. The men are at the mosque, and the children are in bed. The women will be on the roof terrace, gossiping with Mani Aïcha. No one is here to see me walk across the balcony to my bedroom door.

I love the quiet of my room. The privacy. I open the door. Someone has been in. Not just been and left again. My books are gone from the bedside table. And someone has dusted. The cupboard door is open, and my clothes are gone. I go to the wooden box at the end of my bed, where I keep my treasures. An ottoman chest in an Ottoman palace. I already know it will be empty. My treasures don't look special, but they're mine. And precious to me. And then there's the wedding dress I'm going to sell if I get back to England. A backpack is beside the bed. Amal's? My wretched grandmother has moved my sister in here without even asking.

Well, I don't have to share everything. I made the bedding and curtains at the Embroidery School, and I paid for every bead, silk thread and scrap of fabric. They aren't hers to give away. And I saved for six months, from the remnants of my wages, to buy the copper birdcage that hangs from a chain in the window, where I keep Bird, my goldfinch. I have nowhere else to put him, but I pull the curtains from the window. I've embroidered them with tiny mirrors and fold them carefully so that the fabric doesn't snag. Indian embroidery, not Algerian, but a girl from London like Amal won't know the difference. Or appreciate it. My bed cover is made from soft scraps of fabric and decorated with beads and sequins. It isn't comfortable, but it is exotic. I wrap it with the curtains. Grandmother gave me the blue and white scarf that I've draped across the mirror. She told me it belonged to her cousin Hayat, a dancing girl, and that her cousin would have wanted me to have it. It is sheer and soft and lovely, and I have never tried to decorate it. I couldn't do anything to it without ruining it. It is safer here. I leave it for my sister.

I bolt my bedroom door and push against a hinge on my cupboard. A tiled square of plasterboard swings open. Behind the plasterboard there is a room. Dad told me that the room is a secret I mustn't share. Not even Grandmother knows about it. It might have been built during the War of Independence, but I think it's even older than that. Dad said fighters hid here. Men and women who were martyred for us. I pull the cupboard and plasterboard away from the wall. It may well be the best piece of building work that the palace has ever seen, because it is silent and swings high enough to leave no mark on the floor. Inside is a small table with two wooden stools. Another wooden box on the table hides the pretty things I collect for my sewing, away from rats and the thieving fingers of children.

And opposite my piece of plasterboard is an

archway with steps down to a concealed doorway that leads onto the narrow street outside. And to Ali.

CHAPTER TWO

I haven't slept in one of the children's rooms since I was sixteen. There are four divans in here, and there should be plenty of space, but my cousins aren't tidy. There are schoolbooks and magazines piled everywhere, and they've just dumped their clothes on the spare bed. My bed. Nassima has a pile of my things in her arms. She found me on the roof, gave me a hug, and told me it was time for bed. There are times when I'd argue and tell her that I'm a woman now, but I'm weary. And I just want to be peaceful. For everything to be calm. That was why I went up on the roof. You can see the sea from the roof, and it goes on forever and reminds me that I am very little, and my problems are very little. I don't know why it helps to feel insignificant. I don't do insignificant. I do 'Listen to me', 'Look at me', like Grandmother. I'm so like her. Or hope I am. But I won't ever tell her that I admire the way she always does exactly what she wants and says what she wants. No one ever tells her to be quiet.

Nassima pushes the clothes off the bed onto the floor, and hands me my night clothes.

'Don't take it out on the girls. You should have seen their faces when I said you were going to sleep here. They feel very grown up to be sharing with you, so be nice.'

Nassima is always telling me to be nice. I have no idea why. She hugs me for a moment, before stepping backwards and almost falling as her foot catches on the strap of a handbag.

'I ought to take a before photo,' she says.

Nassima knows me. She knows what I'll do. I've got tomorrow off. I'll wash all the clothes before the girls wake up. They'll be stuck in nighties all day, but it's hot and I don't suppose they'll mind. After I've done that, I'll ask Ali, or Uncle Dahkman, to put up some bookshelves, and make hooks for their school bags. I'll see how settled Amal looks but I might whitewash the walls. There are grey fingerprints and one of the little ones has drawn a picture of a flower in crayon, under the window. I miss the television in England. The house makeovers, and garden shows, with designers racing against the clock. They should give me a job. I'd be great!

I lie down on my bed. I'll go clean my teeth in a minute. I cuddle my bundle of clothes and notice my mum's old cardigan. It was her favourite. A baggy old grey thing with little pearl buttons. I put them on when I was twelve, swapping them for the plastic things with four holes. I bought the buttons with my pocket money. She wore it all the time after that. It used to smell like her. That vague musty womanly smell that meant Mum. I rub the edge of the sleeve on the side of my face, and curl up, not worried about nighties or toothpaste. Just remembering.

***

The ideas that I have at bedtime are better imagined than fulfilled; but if I don't get out of bed and do the laundry, I'll have to spend another night in a room scented with eau de teenage girl. Strictly speaking I could include myself in that, but I think I must wash more than they do. It is comforting being here though. Their breathing. The little sounds they make. Maybe I am lonelier than I realised.

Outside the sky is brightening. Clothes lie crumpled across the floor. Bundling them onto my bed, I stumble on a small hedgehog . . . a hairbrush lying in the middle of the floor. I wish I had tongs for their underwear. I'm sure I can't have gathered everything. Tomorrow I'll do the bed clothes and their nightdresses. For today the girls can sit around in their night clothes like a little hareem. Their room is in what was the women's quarters, like mine. These walls will have seen worse.

Using my covers, I bundle the washing together and tie the corners into bunny ears. Coming out of the bedroom I kick at the washing and enjoy the satisfying whoosh of air as it flumps down each set of stairs, at the end of each balcony. We use the kitchen for washing. We use the kitchen for a lot of things. At least the water is warm this early. I grated some soap yesterday, but it's gone, so I grate some more as the sink fills. There's a washing machine in the corner, but it doesn't work. If it was any older you could sell it to a museum. But there's a mangle. Far more useful, and it works during the power cuts. I've never seen a mangle anywhere else in Algiers. Maybe it is unusual, but I don't know. I put my hand in the water to see if I can froth the soap into bubbles, but it just makes the water look scummy, and that's before I've started on the wash. But it's soothing. I'm not a natural lark, but when I get up early and the palace is quiet there is a calm that sinks into me. It's like the house has a soul and the soul likes me. I'm still here, up to my elbows in water, grinding my fists into the clothes in the sink, when I notice she's here. Standing in the doorway. My new sister.

'Can I help?' It's a long time since someone asked me that, but I've nearly finished. She's looking round the kitchen.

'Is there a kettle?' she asks.

'No. We just boil the water up in a saucepan.'

She finds the saucepan and holds it out for a second before she realises she can't get to the sink, because I am still there. She hugs the saucepan and waits. I rinse the last skirt and put it on top of the rest of the washing in the plastic linen basket.

'Coffee?'

I nod. I empty the sink and kick the basket towards the mangle. The water puddles from the basket as I move it, but I ignore it, walk watery footprints across the floor. I put the tin bucket under the mangle and start turning the handle and pushing the first T-shirt between the rollers. I can mop the floor when I finish if it hasn't dried. Amal has filled the saucepan and is trying to turn on the hob. She tries to make the oven spark to light the gas. She presses the knob to see if it clicks, and then she turns the handle to the left to try and make it catch. Reaching across I take the box of matches from the shelf and pass it to her.

She looks at the matches as if they are an exotic species of wood lice.

I take them from her, and as I pull the little box from her grip, she grabs my fingers.

'Your hands. They look really sore. You should use hand cream or something.'

I flick a match on the side of the box and place it next to the burner. The gas catches.

'There are lots of things I should do,' I say.

'I'm not trying to be awkward.'

'I can't afford hand cream.'

'Oh.'

She goes to the washing basket, and picks up the next item, squeezes it over the rest of the washing, and begins to feed it into the mangle.

'Be careful, if you do it too fast it can pull your fingers in and doesn't work so well.' It doesn't take much to make her smile, apparently. She grins at me and carries on with the washing while I get the mugs, and a couple of coffee sachets that have found their way home from the hotel. It's better than the stuff Mani Aïcha gets us from the souk.

'Milk?'

She nods.

When she's finished with the mangle, I pour the dirty water from the bucket into the sink. The water spirals clockwise into the plug hole. I've never had anyone to help me carry the washing up the three tiers of balconies to the roof before, so I get her to carry the coffee instead. I push open the door, and a gush of cool air rushes past us into the palace.

'Oh look, we're in time,' I say. The sun is rising.

We sit together on fluorescent green plastic chairs at a table with a grubby white tablecloth held in place with red and green glass beads. I know nothing about her, but that's okay. It doesn't really matter right now. We watch the sun come up from behind the mountains in the east, across the Bay of Algiers. It really doesn't matter, on the terraced roof, finishing our coffee.

Amal is the first to get up. 'Where are the pegs?'

I pass her a fruit bowl filled with dolly pegs. The split wooden pegs that English school children dress and put on strings in classrooms. I wonder if Grandmother acquired them when she acquired the mangle. We take the clothes, and starting at opposite ends of the washing line, hang them out. The dresses, and coloured skirts. My hijab. We meet in the middle, taking both ends of the red blanket from my new bed. We could have been hanging up washing together for years, because hanging the blanket feels as familiar as a favourite song, and as simple.

She doesn't say a lot. Amal. She sits there, stroking the mug of coffee with her soft manicured little fingertips. It's Uncle Dahkman's mug. Decorated with the words Les Fennecs – the national football team. I've got a mug with sweet peas on. I hide it in the cupboard in the kitchen, behind the haik, at the top in the corner. Nothing is mine here, not really. We don't have much and the lack of things fosters a generosity, but I like the mug. It reminds me of home. I put my mug on the table, and my forearms on the table, tucking my hands towards my body so she can't see them.

We watch the Casbah waking up. Three terraces away a woman settles to feed her baby, uncovering her hair and lifting her face towards the sun. Beyond her two women come to the roof, hanging jeans and T-shirts on the long lines that once carried long white veils and the hooded traditional garments worn by our men. Two little girls in pink school smocks run to kiss one of the women, and a boy calls from the stairs, hurrying his little sisters back inside to eat their breakfast. Minutes later I can hear them in the alley below us, heading towards the French quarter.

How many quarters am I? And made of what? A French mum, and an Algerian dad, but born in England so I've the sort of townie Kentish accent you can cut butter with. The proper sort of butter, straight out the fridge.

'Were you born here?'

A question I don't answer straight away, because it'll be giving her permission to be nosey, and then I will have to ask her a question and be polite and then I will find out more about her. What we have in common. The things we know about Dad. All those things we might end up sharing. And then she will go away, and I will have wasted my time telling her. And I might miss her. I have enough people that I miss already. I don't need more. So I don't answer, and I look at the sun just above the mountains and the way it shines on the sea in the bay. She tries again.

'Do you have to go to work or anything today?' That

question is safer.

'No. It's my day off. I was just going to sit up here for a bit and sew.' Oh, how easy it is to say too much. To add that bit that I didn't mean to add. Now she will ask about the sewing. Except she doesn't. Give her credit for that. There's a plastic box under the table, and I hook my foot behind it, and bring it closer. I don't know whether to open it and show her. But I'm kind of proud of it. And she will see I'm not a complete loser.

I unclip the lid and pick out the bodice I'm working on. There's a moment. When you share that you can do beautiful, make beautiful, a beautiful something from nothing. The person you show changes their expression, and they become intent, and want to touch the beautiful you've made. She does that. She holds out her hand, but then hesitates and looks at my face. I lay it in her hands, like a vicar pressing a communion wafer in a waiting palm, like I'm giving her something sacred. Her mouth is open, and she frowns a little.

'Where did you get this?'

Humph. As if it wasn't mine. As if I'm not clever enough.

'I made it.'

'Oh wow, Rabia.' She holds it close to her face, as if she's short-sighted or long-sighted or, I don't know . . . as if she needs glasses. And she notices things. She really looks.

'There are little bumble bees, and fuchsias . . . and are they irises? They grow here too, don't they?' Her noticing is more frightening than anything else. Because I want to babble about the bumble bee hotel I made with Mum in our back garden, and the half tubs that we screwed either side of the front door each summer with trailing fuchsias dropping red and purple onto the doormat. And she'll see the swallows, and the bunny with its mother, eating grass, next to the daffodils.

'So that's the answer to my question,' she says. 'You weren't born here, were you? You're as English as me.' She passes my sewing back, and turns, looking across the Casbah, cradling her mug.

I thread my little gold-tipped needle with white silk and wait. Trying to decide what to draw with the needle. Waiting for a spark of inspiration.

'What flowers do you like?'

Amal smiles. 'I like campanulas and canterbury bells and . . .'

'Okay.' I shut my eyes, picture them at the base of the wall by the apple tree and start to sew. I went to school in Canterbury, but she doesn't need to know.

'I was born in London,' she says. I shrug. Take it. Leave it. Tell me if you want to, but my ears are straining to hear every breath and syllable.

'Not the middle of London. Greater London. Just outside.'

'I know.' She smiles. Really smiles.

'Yeah. You would know. My . . . our father lived in London when he met Mum. She never told him about me. She kicked him out and never said a word. Just left.'

'She had a lot in common with him then.'

'What?'

'Dad disappears too. Grandmother, Mani Aïcha, says it's because our ancestors were from the Ouled

Naïll.'

'What?'

'The Naïll tribe. From the mountains. The girls used to come into the oasis towns and cities to dance, and when they had enough money in a silver dowry they'd go home, buy some land and choose a husband. They were nomads.'

'So, am I from them too?'

'We're sisters, of course you are.'

'What sort of dancers?'

'A bit like belly dancers. All wiggly bums and twerking.'

Amal lifts her mug and looks at her gently rounded belly. 'I don't think I inherited any of that.'

'They took years learning. They started as little ones and went into the towns as teenagers. They didn't learn in a day.' I try to sound knowledgeable and superior.

'Can you dance like them?'

I lift the embroidery like Amal lifted her mug and look at my own belly with a frown.

'No.'

Amal laughs, with a laugh that smiles up into her eyes and makes the coffee in the mug rise in a wave to the rim. I like her. I like that she isn't fussed about the coffee on her jeans until I remember that it'll be me washing them, and she's used to a washing machine.

I pull the plastic chair away from the table, so that my embroidery is away from my clumsy sister, and thread some little pearl beads onto the silk.

'Who's it for?' she asks.

I stop sewing for a moment, looking up from the

tiny beads.

'The . . . what you're sewing.'

'It's my wedding dress.'

I have her complete attention now.

'But you can't be very old. Seventeen? Eighteen?'

'Eighteen.'

'It's a bit young to get married.'

'Tell Mani that.' The thread frays and I dampen it with my tongue before clamping it between my teeth to pull it straight, licking the end so that it is pointed enough to put more beads on.

'Who are you marrying?'

'Mani is friends with the baker, and he has a son, and they want us to get married.'

'Oh.'

I look up. She's staring at me.

'And do you want to marry this baker's son?' I pick up a clear sequin and start to thread it before the thread frays again, and I reach for my embroidery scissors. Gold-plated scissors with delicate handles shaped like a swan. A present from my mum. Sweet sixteen. I snip the end of the cotton.

'I would marry anyone who could get me away . . .' and I stop. Too much. I didn't want her to know where I was born, and now I'm telling her about Ali. 'I would marry anyone who could get me home to England . . . if I loved them.'

'Do you? Love him?'

'He's my best friend. Stop talking. Let me concentrate, or the pearls will look like our little cousins have been learning to sew.'

She sighs and picks up our mugs. Leaves me to it.

By midmorning the roof and surrounding terraces are hazed with a white heat and the women on the terraces go back indoors. I put my sewing back in the plastic box, and start to unpin the washing from the line, folding it carefully. The blanket is difficult to fold by myself. It would have been easier with Amal.

I take the washing to the bedroom I shared with the girls, and leave the pile folded on the end of my bed. They can sort it out themselves.

CHAPTER THREE

Amti Nassima is sitting at the table with Amal. They look like friends already. I feel that thing that feels like shame, or regret. A pang of something difficult. I've lost my chance. I take some coffee from the pot, and hesitate, standing behind an empty chair.

'Can I?'

Amti Nassima laughs. 'When did you start asking for permission to do anything?'

I sit, less gracious, and dig both my elbows into the table, holding the mug up to my face. Amal has my mug. I make do with the Desert Foxes.

'We're going out,' Nassima says.

Amal and I reply together, 'Are we?'

'Peas in a pod,' Nassima says, and laughs.

'Where to?'

'Why?'

'Mani is tired. She's worn out and I've told her to rest; but she told me to take Amal and show her some of the city.'

I feel excluded. Uninvited.

'Where are we going to go?' Amal asks, her mouth full of pastry, hand under her chin to catch the crumbs.

'You'll see. Rabia, go and fetch some scarves.' Nassima has already covered her hair.

'For me too?' I ask.

Nassima reaches across the table and puts her hand on my wrist.

'You silly girl. Of course, for you too.'

I pull away and tip my coffee into the sink. I will not let her see the tears threatening to crawl down my face. I care. I will not let Amal know how badly I want her to like me; how much I want to feel valued and worth loving.

I come back with my favourite hijabs. One is pale blue, and the other is a lilac shade.

'Do I need this?' she asks.

Nassima answers, 'You'll get less bother as a respectable Arab girl.'

'Bother?'

I smile as I wrap the veil very efficiently and a little too tightly over Amal's hair, tucking it in, and round her neck. Perhaps a bit tight, but scarves don't stay on unless they are tight when you first start wearing them. They are always kind of uncomfortable in the beginning, like your first bra.

'Algerian men are very friendly.'

As we walk through the maze of houses and alleys, I pause occasionally to let her catch up. She isn't used to walking everywhere, and she isn't used to the heat. The fourth time I pause she grabs hold of my arm and makes me wait while she catches her breath.

'I doubt any nice Algerian man could get friendly with a girl who walks as fast as you.'

I giggle. 'You've sussed it. Much better to walk fast round here.'

'And what would your fiancé say?'

Nassima should work for MI6. 'Fiancé, Rabia?'

'No.' Oh why did I tell Amal anything?

'I'm going to go on ahead. I want to pick up some needles.' As I hurry onward, I hear my sister's voice for a moment, 'All the better to stab me with.' And Nassima's reply, 'Rabia seems to be getting the hang of being a little sister, doesn't she?'

'Oh yes.'

I glance over my shoulder, and turning, my face is half hidden in my hijab, so they can't see me sticking out my tongue.

I don't need needles. I don't need to go shopping. I don't need to be a tourist guide for ignorant visitors, and I don't need a sister. I watch their reflections in the shop window, pretending to gaze at silk threads and some pinking shears, but waiting for them to catch me up. Pinking shears. I have some pinking shears, but I don't know how to sharpen them, and the bolt is too loose, so the fabric slips when I try to cut. Useless, like me. They were my mum's. I liked them when I was little. I liked anything pink. I used to sneak them from the sewing box that opened out into wings of little drawers and take them to my bedroom to cut zigzag lines through sheets of thin foam or coloured paper. Mum would find me in my room, cutting shapes, and take the scissors and try to look cross and tell me that paper blunted them. And then she would sit on the floor and draw me onto her lap so that I could show her the coloured bits of paper and explain that the green triangle was an elephant, and the brown square was a banana, and the pink blob was Mani. Gran in her big house. And I took the elephant and made it stomp on the pink blob while Mum hid her smile behind her hands.

The shears were always at the bottom of the sewing box. They were clunky. Too big to fit anywhere else. Mum said that her shears were named after pinks: – vanilla scented flowers with frayed edges – scissors with zigzags to stop the weave fraying. Wish they could stop me feeling frayed round the edges.

Amal is behind me now. She looks to see what I am looking at.

'Can I get you a present? Would you like something? Those scissor things. Or that purse thing for needles. I would like to get you a present.'

'There's nothing I need.'

Oh, liar, liar, pants on fire. I need so many things. I just don't know what they are yet. I hold out my hands to emphasise the nothingness of my needs and seeing the sore knuckles and red cracks where my fingers join the palms of my hand, I pull them back quickly to shove them in my pockets.

'Would you show me how to sew?'

And I turn into my grandmother.

'Who do you think I am? A princess with time to sit sewing all day?'

Nassima rolls her eyes at me, and Amal kind of shrinks in a bit. Gets a bit smaller. Note to self: learn when to shut up.

31

As we arrive in the French town Nassima loosens her scarf, and lets it drop around her shoulders. As if she's only a Muslim in the Casbah.

'I'm going to meet a friend for coffee. Mani wants you to take Amal to Le Jardin du Hamma.'

I can't help the sigh that escapes. It isn't taking Amal that annoys me. It is that Mani is taking control again. I wanted to go to the harbour. I wanted to sit outside my favourite café. Days off are too precious to waste, but obedient granddaughter that I am, I walk off in the direction of the gardens. You kind of know when someone isn't following. I turn round. Amal takes half a step as if she's going to follow Nassima, and then I see her look at me, and she suddenly chooses to hurry to catch up.

Amal sees everything. She doesn't look at her feet like me. I keep watching her as we walk. Pretend that I'm looking to cross the road. Looking over my shoulder if I hear a noise so that I can glance at her face. I've been here for two years, but it might as well be forever. I haven't really seen Algiers. Being with Amal is like taking the little cousins to the park. They still see things: ants, beetles. They're awed by the butterflies and watch the house martins in the cracks in the walls, and the clouds of goldfinch that whirl above the Casbah. Occasionally Amal opens her mouth as if she wants to ask something. I've got to try harder. Got to be 'nice', like Nassima said.

'What's that?' she says.

On the hill in front of us, visible from the whole city, is a tower. Triple struts, that seem suspended, rising together to the sky.

'It's a memorial. To the martyrs of the FLN,' I say.
'Who?'

'Don't you know anything? Didn't you read about this place? Open a book? Google it?' I don't bother waiting for an answer. It's obvious that she hasn't. 'The FLN were our "resistance". The Martyrs Monument remembers them. Lots of them died. Mani Aïcha was one of them. Not one of the dead ones. One of our soldiers.' I've got her interest. But anything I say gets her interest. Why does she keep trying so hard? She has stopped walking, so I need to stop walking too.

'Mani was extraordinary. Really brave. She was one of the women who planted bombs in the cafés in the European Quarter. But I suppose she had more reason than most to hate them. The French.'

'Oh.' She puts her hand up. Covers her mouth. Eyes wide. 'A terrorist.'

'A freedom fighter. No different from the Home Guard in England or the Resistance in France when the Germans invaded during the Second World War.'

'Maybe.'

'Not maybe. Mani's a hero. They put a bomb in her bag, and she put it in a café.'

'God, you make it sound clinical. The bag? Is that why she always has her bag with her? The black bag.'

'Dad gave it to her. He told her he bought it in Harrods and told her that the Queen has one just like it. Dad is full of shit. He probably bought it in Asda and pinched the plastic Harrod's bag.' Amal looks like she would have asked more about Mani but asks about Dad instead.

'I don't really know anything about him. Mum

didn't want to tell me much. Later on, she couldn't remember much. She was ill for a long time.'

I want to ask about her version of our dad, but if I show I'm interested she will tell me more, and then I will listen and get to know her, and then I'll wake up one day and find that I care but that she's gone. And I'll be alone again, but it will be worse. This loneliness.

'You really don't plan on sharing about him, do you? I can't take him away from you, Rabia. He's yours. I had a stepfather. I grew up with a man in the house who loved my mum and was a dad in all the right ways. Except for the sperm cell at the beginning. I don't need your dad, our dad. I just want to know who he was.'

'He's not dead.'

'Dahkman told me he doesn't know–'

'Don't talk about him like he's gone forever. He'll come back. Our ancestors were from the Ouled Naïll and Mani's father was a Tuareg. Travellers. Nomads. He can't help himself. He'll go away, but he always comes back. Mani told me that he was gone for five years once. That was when he met your mum. He only came back because she kicked him out and his visa expired.'

'She never saw him again.'

'Why not?' I ask.

Amal shakes her head, and her lips tighten before she replies, 'Some things are private.'

CHAPTER FOUR

This is the thing. Something strangers don't get. Algiers is divided in two. Like an apple. One half whole. One half rotten. And you have to know who you are, where you belong, before you know which bit to bite. The French thought the Casbah was the rotting part. They've a point. The plaster's falling off the walls. The tiles are faded, and the balconies above the street are unstable. If you walk through the alleys, be careful what you walk under. Careful where you step. Hold your skirt or haik so that it won't brush against the rubbish sacks that are never collected. You need perfume on the edge of your scarf to hold to your face in the really bad bits, but to us it is the French part that is all decay. Decayed morals. The past that we can't quite shed that arrived with the graceful well-built buildings: the post office, the wide streets. If you look carefully, you can see scars from the Civil War. Smashed circles where bullets hit creamy plaster. Like they tried to kill the White Lady, our city, too. There's a humming undercurrent of disillusionment and loss. I couldn't tell you if any war has ever been won here. Can you win a war? Maybe wars are never won. Unless you're English and think you can save the world. Or worse, American and think you can rule it.

There are girls on the beaches whose bikinis are smaller than the bits of lace they call underwear; while girls like me pretend not to look at the lingerie: the pretty lace, and matching knickers. We pretend to stick our noses up as we walk past the lingerie in the store, unless no one is nearby when we pause, and wonder who would bother to sew those little pleats and embroider flowers onto scraps that no one should see. In the French part you'll see a girl walking with a boy and holding hands, but down the alleys and through the wrecked arches beyond, the girls walk together in little scented clouds of respectable femininity. I can't see our lives as the rotten part. They look more wholesome, those girls, with their grins and glances shining like lamps at sunset.

The shops with Parisienne fashions and finger smears on the wide windows can't compare with the vegetable stalls with fruit displayed so perfectly in rows, and the street vendors whose smug smiles know that their food is the best in Africa. You've never tasted choukchouka until you've eaten it standing in the marketplace of the Casbah cupping the small dish beneath your chin so that it doesn't drip from your mouth, to stain your haik.

I'd prefer to show Rabia the souk rather than the gardens, but I know why I've been told to come here. We pass under the black sign with its gold letters. Le

Jardin d'Essai u Hamma is written in gold above the entrance.

'Mani wanted me to bring you here. These are the botanical gardens.'

She stands for a moment, looking at the avenue of palms that lead to the sea. The palms are tall, straggling things. In the browning photographs in the antique shop, they are better proportioned. Tidier. The gardens are beautiful, and well-tended but the high palms have passed their best, like onions gone to seed.

'Why did she want me to come here?'

'Because of the English Garden. Le Jardin Anglais.'

'It doesn't look very English,' she says, but follows me obediently, under the stretching branches of the trees, until we come to the mossy damaged statues.

They aren't attractive things. Very solid. Women with heavy headdresses and layers upon layers of clothing. One of the women is holding up a scarf. It's the same sort of scarf as the one in my bedroom but there is nothing bright and translucent about the statue. Another woman is holding out her arms under her own dancer's veil. I pull at Amal's sleeve, moving her on. 'These are special, but they aren't the ones I want you to see.'

We walk a little further into the trees and there is a statue of two more women, standing close together.

'Mani brought me here all the time when I was little. She would be very sad and tell me the same thing each time we came. She would say that her mother, our great grandmother, had been a dancer like these, and had dressed like this. Then Mani would tell me not to wait for things. Not to wait to be happy. We must live now. Be happy here. And if we have sisters, we should remember that they are very precious, and hold them very dear to us.' I never understood why she would go on about sisters when I don't have . . . didn't have one. 'Do you think she knew about you, Amal?'

Amal shakes her head, 'She couldn't have.'

'Remember the statues, because one day I'll tell you about Mani's mother and this will make sense.'

'Can't you tell me now?'

'It's a long story. Not for today. I had to wait for years until I heard all of it.'

If she won't tell me why her mother left Dad, she can wait for my story. Mani's story.

Amal opens her mouth to ask more, but I stand and turn and brush the dust from my skirt, duty fulfilled. I walk fast, so that she won't have the breath to talk; but when I look back, she hasn't moved, and she looks pale.

'The heat's making me dizzy. Please stop.'

'What's wrong with you?'

'I'm not used to the heat. Can we stop for a drink somewhere? Or something to eat?'

I lead her to the café in the gardens and order crêpes. We don't talk. I pretend it is a companionable silence, but it is stiff with everything I don't want to say and the things she won't tell me.

The ice-cold hibiscus cordial washes the dryness from my mouth, and I watch her eating. She's miles away. Somewhere else. I clatter my fork on the plate. I want her attention. She's crunching the ice cubes from her glass and the noise makes her jump but seeing my empty plate she picks up her bag, and pushing her chair back gets to her feet. So we walk back to the entrance. There's a taxi just outside the gardens, and she raises her hand, and it slows to a stop. I want to tell her that I can't pay, but the air-conditioned interior is bliss so for once I keep my mouth shut. She'll have to pay. She's got money. Well, more money than me.

I'm lost in myself in the taxi. I shut my eyes and pretend to be asleep. I don't want to share Dad with her, but I want to wring out everything she knows about him. The details. Anything she knows about what makes him tick. Any clue as to who he is, so that I can understand where he went. Why he left. I thought I knew him so well, but that person, that version of Dad, wouldn't have just gone and left. My version of Dad loved me more than anyone else.

I open my eyes when she speaks. Pretend to wake.

'My Mum told me he used to go missing,' she says. 'He went for four days once and didn't contact her. He didn't go to work, and she couldn't find him anywhere. After four days he came back. He had taken some sort of drug and spent three days in Bart's Hospital in oblivion. I think I am like him. That I've got that bit of him in me too.'

'He's been gone for two fucking years, Amal.' That stops her. But now I've stopped her I wonder what she means. She ignores me and carries on anyway.

'I've gone missing too.'

So I'm right. I can't trust her. She'll leave. When she's ready she'll go, and I will still be here, with Grandmother, and be abandoned all over again. I know she wants me to ask, or think I know. So I shut my eyes, turn my face away. Wait for the brief journey to end.

We arrive back at the edge of the Casbah, and I get out, walk away. Leave her to pay. I walk ahead, making sure she can see me because I'm not that much of a bitch, but far enough so that she can't talk. I am so bloody scared. Of her. Of everything. I can see her behind me, in the glass of the baker's shop. In the little tiled mirrors where I buy fish. I even wait. Just enough so that she doesn't need to walk quite so fast, but I judge the distance and her pace so that when she is close enough to talk, I take off, almost running, to stay out of range of her words.

I push hard against the door of the palace, grit my teeth at the metallic scraping as it opens, and head straight to my room. On autopilot. I shut the door behind me and screw up my face. Like squeezing all the sharpness from a half lemon. It's only when the door pushes against my back, and I open my eyes that it really closes in on me. I'm in my room, but it's Amal's room now, and I'm trapped. She'll think I've come here to be with her, but I've come to get away. How did I get to be so stupid, when I spend all my time treading on sharp eggshells round Grandmother? If I keep on thinking about eggs and lemons, I'll turn into a meringue. Fluffy and sweet and bitter and sharp, and the biscuit bit of all the things that matter will get left behind on the plate.

She sticks her head round the door. And smiles. Like she's pleased I'm there.

'I've come to feed Bird,' I say. There's a little tin on the windowsill with black seeds in, and I tip a small handful into the plastic cup on the side of the cage.

'Is he tame?' I look at her. I don't feel tame. I don't want Bird to be tame. I want to punch something. I fist my fingers into my palms.

'No. If you open the cage, he'll be gone. Dad bought him. I've had him two years and feed him and talk to him; but he'll never be tame. If you let him go, that'll be it. He'll throw himself into the biggest bit of sky he can find and won't look back.' And I want to add, 'like me'. But I don't. Because that would mean I'd be like my dad, and like Amal, and I don't know if I can cope with finding them inside me. And I don't know what I'd do if I was free.

I feed Bird and leave the room, climbing the last stairs to the terraced roof, silent, barefoot, to kneel beside the crumbling wall. Like a child at the communion rail, I put one hand on top of the other; but then lean forwards and rest my chin on my hands. I look towards the bay, over and across the Casbah. I watch the women gathering their washing in the last minutes of the evening, and my gaze passes over the rooftops and pauses at the baker's terrace. There is an archway, and I can see a shadow . . . a shape in the darkness, that writhes. Its outline brushing higher and across and back into darkness. I watch. Wondering who it is. I've seen lovers on the terraces before. What is it about love that makes them think they are invisible? I continue watching, and as night falls, I see the shape separate in two, and I see Ali. And I see Saïed. I raise myself higher, lifting from my haunches so that I'm kneeling upright. Saïed sees me, and pulls Ali's shoulder, as if he'd drag him back into the archway, as if he could hide him, but when Ali looks towards me, he smiles when he sees it's me, and puts his fist over his heart, and puts his hand to his lips, and blows me the kiss on his fingertips. Saïed is silent. He looks from Ali to me and back again to Ali. And Ali puts his fist over his heart, and his hand to his lips, and blows his second kiss to Saïed.

I always knew Ali was gay. Somehow. But seeing him with Saïed makes it real. And gay in theory is not the same as seeing Ali and Saïed kissing in a corner. I resent it. Not because Ali is mine . . . but then I know that that is exactly it. For Ali's secret has always been our secret, and we yearned for the same thing; but he has beaten me to it. He has found that thing. That elusive thing that I want. He's left me behind, like everyone else. The odd little bit of twisted confused citrus sharpness in me is angry because to the outside world Ali has always been mine.

CHAPTER FIVE

Amal doesn't come downstairs. She doesn't notice the noise as the family gathers, or the laughter of the little girls racing to see who can get the most dishes onto the table to please Grandmother. So I go and find her. I stand outside the door to her or my room, not knowing whether to knock or not, and then decide to. Three raps. I stick my head round the door, and halt. She's asleep. In my bed. Her bag abandoned on the floor. Her feet still in her sandals on top of my covers.

I tap her shoulder.

'It's time to eat.'

She blinks like a little owl, and slides her feet to the floor, yawning.

'I'm sorry. I didn't mean to fall asleep, but it was cool, and I lay down for a moment, and here you are.'

As she sits up a cahier, a French style exercise book, falls from a fold of the bed covers and slips to the floor. She doesn't notice and takes the bowl I've brought her, and the glass of squash.

'What are you doing with that?'

'Nothing. Just looking. I wanted something to read, but I don't understand any of it.'

I pick up the book. It's the top one from a little pile on my bookshelf.

'It's our story. I was a child when I wrote them out. Mani wanted me to learn Tamezight and Arabic, and Dad wanted me to improve my French, so they made me go and sit with Amti Fatima, who was kind of Mani's mum. Amti Fatima would tell me the stories, and I would write them how the Tamezight sounded, and then later Dad would make me write in Arabic and French. Each line of text written three times in a different language. Dad wanted me to learn Arabic, but Mum made him promise that I wouldn't learn Arabic from the Koran unless I wanted to, and I suppose I didn't, so they decided to get me to listen to Amti Fatima's stories instead.'

'Can you still read them?'

'You don't have hours and hours of lessons for months of every year, and then forget it all. I can speak Tamezight and Arabic like a stall keeper in the souk, but my French isn't so good. They were less worried about me learning that.'

'Could you read them to me?' she says.

I look at my cahier, marked with a large 1 in the top right corner, and realise that I want to read them too. It is so long since Fatima told me the stories, and I want to remember them. It was hard work, and painful, but sitting with Amti Fatima had always been the best part of the day, because she was affectionate, and gentle, and very patient with me. So I open the book and I'm there again, by the fireside in a camp outside Bou Sâada, with Amti Fatima and all the women who came before us.

I start to read aloud.

When I was a young woman, I believed that this story was mine. My joys. My happiness. My grief. My pain. As I reach the end of all my journeys, I understand that my story ebbs as yours flows and if I am able to tell you what happened to us then you can add it to your own stories and it will become part of you, as it is part of me. If I add it to your stories, then my story will be remembered after I am gone.

I make no apology that this is a story of the women of our tribe. Men think that we ornament their lives, but I believe that it is the men who decorate ours. It is the women of our tribe who pass on our line and our blood to our daughters, and our possessions aren't taken from us when we are widowed or remarry. They are held, like poems and songs, waiting for daughters to take them into the future.

You are a child of the tribe of the Naïll people, the Ouled Naïll. We come from the Hautes Plaines, and the Naïll mountains. Sometimes we are viewed with suspicion, and sometimes we are despised. People who can live inside themselves without need for a place or belongings are feared the world over. The travellers, the nomads, the gypsies. The Ouled Naïll, and the Tuareg. Maybe it is our freedom that is fearsome, or our understanding that nothing belongs to us that brings fear. Not even our bodies belong to us. They are no more than dust and sand. But our souls, we carry our souls forever.

My soul was born into a nomad, wandering the deserts and the scrublands and sheltering in the mountains that carry our name. Our low wide tents were always filled with light and air until darkness came when the soft blankets and rugs under the red and black striped canvas covered the night. In the early morning I would go to the edge of the camps watching the shepherds leading their goats and sheep, calling them by their names, and when the sun began to drop from the height of its pathway, I would watch the men tending their camels, and the young men training their camels to race across the sands, raising clouds and dirt that turned the watching world to dust.

After dark the fires lit the night, and my dreams came running to the sound of the flat thin Naïlli drums and long pipes that accompanied the singing of love songs as our women danced, making the shadows twist and turn from the firelight. I longed to see my own shadow dance but my mother, Zohra, would laugh and hug me in her arms, wrapping me in blankets she had woven from the wool spun in the tents in the heat of the day.

Now, strangers, foreigners, call them what you will, value gold, but we value silver more, because it holds the moon in it. When you have travelled in this country you will soon understand that the moon is so much more beautiful than the sun that burns us. The moon is our witness, for she watches us at our most vulnerable. She sees us in our lovers' arms, hears our whispers at night, and finds us sleeping. I miss the moon. These eyes of mine will never see the moon again.

My mother told me that I was born when the moon

was full and bright in the sky, and that it was harvest time. There was a good harvest that year, and she had had plenty to eat while she carried me. The camels had bred well, and so had the women. Most of the babies survived that year. The gods of the mountains, the sand and the sky and the storms blessed the year, and it was a good time to be a little Naïlliyat, a Naïlli girl.

The outsiders think that we women are only dancers, and the French thought that we were whores. The word prostitute was stamped on our cards when the French issued them, and they forgot that we danced freely, and took our lovers generously as they in turn were generous to us.

Seven harvests after I was born my sister's time of dancing came. She was lovely to watch. Her breasts just blooming, her eyes wide and clear as a well in an oasis. She could make her hands dance like goldfinches and swallows above her head, while her feet drummed in time with the drummer's beat. I watched, longing to join in, but my mother would pause, distracted for a moment, to look at me, and say that life had other blessings for girls like me, and return to Jamila's lessons; but I longed to be Jamila's sister-dancer. Our women dance in pairs, holding the ends of our blue-white scarves, jiggling our breasts and sweeping our hips in sensuous circles above the neat black shoes on our feet. Jamila was lovely when she danced, and when she was old enough – the year her moon times started – she was taken with her sister-dancer, our cousin Hayat, and prepared to journey to Bou Saâda after the harvest.

I watched, captivated, as Jamila's long dark hair was brushed and pulled into thick plaits, coiled at the sides of her lovely face under the large turban like headdress. I was given the job of placing the bobbing ostrich feathers in the bands that held it in place. Her eyes were lined with kohl, and her hands were painted with henna flowers and a week before we set off a traveller took an ink the colour of indigo and tattooed our faces with the point of a tiny knife. The tattoos tell stories too, but even the women who still bear them have forgotten the meanings of their symbols.

Our Mother, Zohra, had been a dancer, and it was obvious that Jamila was her blood and bone. Some of our women laughed at me, for I have always been short and plain, and they said that I was a swapped child, put in my mother by a djinn who had hidden in her womb when she was sleeping. My mother was known for the wonderful pearls that she wore, and they said that it was the pearls that had attracted a water demon, lost far from the rivers and seas, but enough pitying, and enough of their jealousy and spite. Because Zohra was my mother, and we girls had no father, I was allowed to travel to Bou Saâda with them. Bou Saâda . . . the name still lifts the breath in my body . . . our Place of Happiness.

If you live travelling then a journey never takes long, for everything is a journey and the destinations become less important, but I craved that journey and that place. I had never seen the dancers dressed to perform and earn their silver dowries. I would have walked in front of the troupe of dancers and musicians and hurried them with bright woven camel ropes if only I had known which way to go. It was an anguish to be told to wait, to come back, to walk with my mother beside our camels.

When I first saw Bou Saâda it was an emerald set within pearls. The oasis fed gardens and the buildings in the Medina reflected the sunlight. I had never seen gardens or cultivated flowers. Some of them were large and bright, all different, and some smelt like nothing but grass, but others pushed perfume sweeter than my sisters' into each breath I took. My favourites were the tiny white stars of the jasmine that scented the evenings there. I had no coins or headdress, but twisted the long stems of jasmine, and made a crown of flowers to wear in my hair. How can I tell you of my happiness? It was a bubbling fury of joy erupting from me. It was the elation of a girl who is smiled at by a boy. The thrill of first seeing the sea that goes on forever from the shore. And it was more. It was more than all these things to be in Bou Saâda.

We waited until the evening for our procession, making camp, each with our job. I found water and fed the camels before finding sticks, shrubs and camel dung to burn on our fires. My uncles pitched our tents, and the women baked bread on metal discs in shallow pits that they dug into the sandy soil. My mother let me make the zviti, and I helped her pound the bread into the spicy orange sauce.

When we had settled, my sister was dressed in the heavy layered skirts, and cotton blouse and bodice of a dancer. I watched; each layer placed deliberately. I have heard that the Catholic nuns in the city pray as they dress, placing each item of clothing into the ritual of their day. There were no prayers for dressing Jamila, but I never saw a ritual more lovely. It was the ritual of a bride, and perhaps that was what she was; but I didn't understand what she joined herself to that day. I have never really understood that, and she is not here to explain.

The dancing girls were helped onto the camels amid laughter and teasing. The singers started whispering and humming the tunes of the love songs, and the drummers started twisting their wrists as if their fingers were impatient to join in. I was made to walk behind with my mother, and the women who were too old to dance. I had not noticed until then, always straining ahead, that there was a man wearing a shesh who walked with us. His shesh – a veiled turban – was the colour of the sky just before full night, and although I could only see his eyes, they were the merry eyes of a man who knows what it is to be joyful.

I pulled at the edge of his garment. 'Why are you veiled?'

His eyes were too young to wrinkle with his smile, but he held out a hand, and answered me, considering my question with great dignity. 'My father said it helps to keep the sand out of a man's mouth when we are travelling, but my mother told me that men must wear our veils to keep the evil ones away.'

I looked up puzzled. 'Only the men? Don't your women need to keep the evil ones away too?'

He shrugged and laughed quietly at my question. 'Our women are like yours, little sister. They don't wear veils.'

'Why not?'

His eyes were kind at my persistence. 'So that we can see your beautiful faces.'

I stopped my questions to think about the answer. It

sounded like he meant that I had a beautiful face as well.

There is something in every little girl that waits, ready to bloom like a rosebush in a watered pot, that longs to be beautiful; and there is a heart in every little girl that longs to beat in the breast of a woman who is loved and appreciated. The place inside that holds those longings came alive that day.

'What is your name?'

'I am Abdulkader.'

I entered Bou Saâda balanced high on the shoulders of Abdulkader. If we were asked to choose the perfect moment of our lifetime – a moment to never forget – a moment to return to, that we could live again, I would choose that moment, and be just that child, sitting on his shoulders with jasmine blossoms in my hair, the smallest part of a procession of dancers.

I don't remember much about where my sister danced that night. I was a child, maybe six years old, and I am allowed to forget, but grateful for what I remember. I do remember that there were campfires, and that I felt drowsy as I curled up in the circle of my mother's lap to watch the girls. I had settled to sleep so many times in her arms that it would have been easy to turn towards her and shut my eyes; but as soon as Jamila and Hayat started to dance my weariness left. I saw my sister dancing full of joy, turned in completely to herself so that she danced . . . how do I tell you? I think my mother said it best. She said that Jamila danced like no one was watching, and then smiling she said that I danced as if everyone was watching, and that was why I would never be a dancer.

Jamila was joy dancing between the campfires. I was

hunger. Aching to be like her. Longing to be grown up and part of her world. My mother hugged me closer and whispered, 'There are other things for you, little one. You have a different place in that which is to come,' and she kissed the top of my head with its jasmine crown.

There are moments that last forever. There are moments that we should remember deeply, so that even when our sight is clouded, and the sun no longer shines into our eyes we can draw the pictures and sounds and music into the place where our minds can still see. Jamila has always danced in the place where my mind sees. All the little perfect steps, with her hands above her head, so that her breasts were lifted, and her limbs seemed longer, and her hips rounder, but it wasn't that we saw. It was her face. I wonder if it was a child loving a sister, but I think it was different. I think it was a completion, a consummation, as if one of the lovers of the gods of the sea and the sky and the sand and the storms had entered her and was dancing through her.

Until she and Hayat danced there was the gentle whispered talk and laughter of men as they smoked and leaned back on their elbows to watch. When Jamila danced, they sat forward, and the only sound was the drum and the pipe and the singer's deep voice reminding the girls of the stories that they told. The men who watched fell quiet and there was stillness, as if everyone but Jamila and Hayat held their breath. My mother's arms tightened around me as we watched.

After the dancers had finished, and the hum of talking had resumed I saw my sister talking to a young man, a soldier. He tightened and unclenched his hands around his beret repeatedly as he talked to her, as if he was a child trying not to reach out and take an extra pastry from the dish. Another man came behind him, and whispered in his ear, pushing some money into the pocket of his uniform before pushing his elbow into the young man's back so that he stumbled against Jamila. He was full of miserable apologies, but Jamila laughed, and without thinking put her hands on his, stilling them. She turned to my mother and asked a question with her gaze and a slight movement of her hands.

'Can I?'

My mother lifted her shoulders slightly. 'You make your own choices now.'

Jamila took the young man's hand and drew him away from us, and away from the faint shadows of the embers and torches where the dancers had been, into the darkness beyond our sight.

I pause, glancing at my sister. Amal is asleep, and she has curled up, her arm round her pillow. I take a thin crimson ribbon and put it in the cahier to mark our place, before leaving her to sleep.

CHAPTER SIX

I breathe deeper when I'm away from the family. When I run through the fresh morning in the alleyways on my way to work, hidden in my haik. Except I'm not hidden at all when I wear it, because the women here look at height, and width, pace and posture. Europeans can't see it. In Algeria we notice the details of a cousin's feet or the shopkeeper's basket and how she holds it in the crook of her elbow. We see the things that no one sees in England, when you know someone is someone because of the colour of her hair, and the way it is pulled back in a ponytail, or just recognizing a face. When the little crocheted veils cover our faces, we see the pattern in the crochet instead. We notice the stitches. Our veils aren't a way of hiding, because when you are used to them, when you wear them, you realise that you can see everything else. You hear more of what is being said. You work harder to understand, as if a naked face is a laziness compared to the luxury of a veil. And the veils talk. The haik says, 'I am an Algerian woman. I come from the body of Algerian women. I wear a haik that keeps the dust from me, that shines white, so that you know I launder it with bleach.' The hijab says, 'I am a woman who prays. A woman who knows what she believes and is unashamed. I cover my hair, and you don't know if I am bald or if my hair falls to my feet. So you get to look at who I am instead. Like the Sunday School God from England, who looks on the heart.'

As I reach the French city, I fold my haik, and put it in my basket, because the boss in the sewing rooms thinks the veils are about subservience. She won't let us wear them. Grandmother prefers us veiled. Please one, then hide the haik. Please the other.

My mind is full. Full of this sister. Full of Ali. I know Saïed. I've always known him. He lives just across from our terrace. We made paper aeroplanes to throw to him when we were five maybe, or six. Until an Amti caught us playing, caught me. As I over-leaned and inhaled that breath of falling. And as I started to tumble, she reached me. Held my wrist and caught me. I don't know why Ali was blamed, but he was, and my shoulder was dislocated. Amti took me downstairs to Dad and in rapid incomprehensible Tamezight yelled at him and threw me into his lap. I still wonder if she said, 'This stupid girl of yours thinks she has wings. This idiot child thought she could fly. Where were you? Why don't you look after her yourself? Take some responsibility for her. You can't come here every summer and just dump her on us.' Or maybe she said, 'Take Rabia to the Clinic. I pulled her arm out of her socket.' Because she had. And it hurt as if someone had shoved the bottom of a hot saucepan into it.

Before he took me to the clinic Dad smacked the top of my leg. Hard enough to leave his handprint.

And then I went to the clinic, and a young female doctor, without a smile, took my arm and twisted it back into place with a neat pop. No smile. No pain relief. She looked at me without sympathy before turning to Dad and said, 'She won't try that again in a hurry.'

My arm was strapped for a fortnight, and Dad took me home to Kent where Mum fussed over me when she saw my bandages, until Dad told her what had happened. I didn't know till then that the pink on a face really can drain to white like a line passing down it. Her hands shook when I went to sit on her lap. After I went to bed, I heard her shouting at him. Like Amti had shouted at him, which was ridiculous, because he was perfect. Summer was over, but I didn't mind that year because I was glad to be home; and Mum took two weeks off work to look after me. Perhaps it was damage limitation. She watched me like a hawk and made me rest. I've never been someone who rests. Dad says – always said – I get that from Grandmother.

Enough. I've daydreamed all day but need to concentrate. If I prick my fingers any more today, I'll be back darning tea cloths. The sewing room is hot and airless today. The air-con isn't working, and the sewing mistress is here, showing the new girls how to hem the white tablecloths.

CHAPTER SEVEN

He's waiting for me outside the hotel. Ali. He's leaning against the wall pretending to look like a film star; but he is a big shambles of a man. Except for his face. He has one of those faces that makes your heart pause for a moment. As if it has been caught and held tight in someone's hand like a surgical scene in a dodgy episode of *Holby City*. I'm grateful he's gay; because if he wasn't he would be off with some gorgeous little bird of a woman and I'd be watching their backs as they walked away. Except he's a brother, really. Not for romance, or marriage, and definitely not for sex. But there is always joy when I see him. Well, normally. Unless I am in a really shitty mood. Which I suppose is fairly often. But meeting me outside the hotel is always a good move. I love the coming out of the stuffy sewing room, into the fresh wide air. I associate leaving work, and freedom with the smell of cigarettes in the café near the hotel. It sometimes makes me want to go to a table and beg a cigarette off someone; but when the escapee, Rabia, calms herself down I realise that I really do hate the stench of cigarettes in the confines of a room, in my hair, on my clothes. Madame, in the sewing room, once sacked a girl on the spot for coming in smelling of smoke. Madame told her that she made couture, not brothel wear. The girl should have known better. We shower when we arrive at work and are forbidden perfumes. So, our day is scented with linen, cotton and lace straight from the bolt. Or tea towels and tablecloths straight from the laundry.

Ali, when I get close to him is a jumble of olfactory sensations. He gives me a completely inappropriate, married-by-teatime hug and I stand in his arms for a moment, and he smells of yeast and flour and sweat and shampoo. He realises what I'm doing, because I've done it before and pushes me off.

'Get off, Rabia. Stop sniffing.' His voice is pinched. I look up at him. Five feet have a long way to go to look up at six foot two, when you're standing right next to it. Something's up. His face tight, his eyes bloodshot.

'Tell me then. What's happened?' So he pushed me off, but now he pulls me back in.

'Saïed's uncle saw us.'

A parent might hide it. A brother might. But not an uncle, full of the silent exquisite jealousy that is bred between brothers over their children. And I know Saïed's uncle. Full of smoke and chewing tobacco, and his own importance. Oh God. He'll tell someone.

'What did he see?' I hope it is a hug. A smile. Merely a touching of hands on passing in the alleyways of the Casbah.

'He found us in Saïed's room.'

Shit. Double shit.

'Doing what? Rolling about on the bed?'

Ali doesn't answer and doesn't look at me.

That's a yes then.

'Oh, Ali.'

Two of the girls from the sewing room choose to walk past just at that moment. One bumps into me, pushing me closer, into Ali's arms. Both girls turn to smile and look, walking backwards for a few steps before carrying on home.

'What are you going to do? What's his uncle going to do?'

'He's done it. He told Saïed's dad, said he'd call the police. Saïed'll end up in prison. We'll both end up in prison. And what will they do to us? Rabia. Please help us. Please help me.'

'How?' I ask, but I know how.

If I marry him everyone will know that they were just foolish. Just messing about. Making their mistakes together rather than destroying my virtue, or the virtue of another girl. Not really gay. Not really in love. Not so desperately drawn to each other that they risked everything without the will to stop themselves. I won't answer now. Because I'll keep my word when I decide. Because I am a Kateb. Because I am my grandmother's.

'Let's go and see Uncle Dahkman,' I say. Dahkman spent years in England. He has a broader view, and he won't shout. 'We'll tell him that . . . we'll tell him something.'

I pass Ali my shopping basket and reach into it for my haik. Another costume. Another Rabia.

We walk back to the Casbah. Slowly. Planning quietly. Silent. We walk up the smooth steps, past the Grand Mosque. Ali turns his face from the Mosque, as if The Prophet is inside watching him walk past.

'Where's Saïed?'

Ali reaches out for my hand.

'He went with his uncle. I left. I ran. I should have stayed, Rabi. I shouldn't have just left. I should have said something and . . .'

He lifts my hand, brushing it across his eyes, held in his hand, so that I feel his tears across my knuckles.

I squeeze his hand, and we carry on walking.

We are nearly home. Near Saïed's house, close to the Palace of Birds, when I hear shouting. Some men are standing in the doorway of Saïed's house and looking upward. Saïed's uncle stands in the middle. He is beating on the door with both fists. He is shouting about honour. About family. About protecting the women of his family from filth. Ali and I stand at the corner. We need to pass to get me home, but we can't pass them. The hidden doorway in the little alley is close but I can't get there without being seen. And then we look up. Ali looks up and sees Saïed standing on the edge of the terrace. And Saïed sees us. He touches his hand to his heart, to his lips, and then shouts above the mob that is gathering.

'It was me. It was all me. I love him. But Ali loves her. Ali would never leave her. I tried to make him love me, to show him.'

The people below have fallen silent.

'I saw them,' Saïed's uncle says. 'I am not a fool.'

But Saïed has gone. He isn't standing there on the

roof anymore. The men in the street below look at each other, wondering what to do. What happens next? Sheep wondering whether they are to be led by the shepherd or herded by a dog. And then a gasp, a collective intake of breath, and I look up, just in time, to see Saïed running. Reaching towards the edge of the roof, and launching himself, arms outspread, his silhouette dark against the sky. For a moment I believe it. I believe that he can fly. That he is flying. That he is going to soar, and escape, and find a way to live. And then a sound comes from him. 'All . . .' his voice trails off. And I can see his face. He is close enough that I can see the exhilaration replaced by despair as he falls, reaching towards his lover. I shouldn't have turned my face, because then I wouldn't have heard him land. Or it wouldn't be imbedded in my memory forever as a sound. The crack and squelch of a snail underfoot. Except it wasn't a snail. It was him.

When I look back Saïed is lying on the ground. His mouth closes for a moment and opens again, and then he is completely still. A pool of blood growing from beneath his head trickles down the uneven tiles towards the watchers at the doorway of his home.

I try to stop Ali running forwards. He lands hard on his knees beside Saïed. I try to pull at his hands so that he doesn't get blood on him. I try and look like a woman in despair and love. A woman protecting her man, but the others have turned towards us, and Saïed's uncle is screaming at us, at Ali. He's screaming words that nice girls shouldn't know and don't use. He stands over us, and slaps Ali hard across the face. Hard like the crack of a bread crock when it drops and breaks. And the men are coming closer to us. Not us. Ali.

I feel someone behind me, pulling at my haik, reaching to grab my hair. Hands on the tops of my arms that push past the woman while her hands clutch at me, so that I am pulled back, and half carried to the door of the Palace of Birds. Pushed through it. And the door is slammed behind me, closing out the shouting and screams and the iron-scented blood trickling past the door. It's Dahkman. My uncle. He came out and pulled me away. Brought me home.

I'll cry later. I'll find some comforting arms to sob in. But right now, I need to work out what it was that I saw. What happened. What it means. Ali and I will sit in the courtyard, and . . . oh God, Ali. Ali is still out there.

'Mani!' I scream her name. She will know what to do. If Dahkman goes out there he'll just be a man with the mob, and they might turn on him. He rescued me and can't go back out there. But Mani. She'll know. She'll do something. I'm sure she'll find a way to do something. She comes, stomping up each step. Small and determined as a train moving up a mountainside. And she sees me, and she stops, her mouth dropping open.

'Ali's out there. They're attacking Ali.' She looks at me. My hair half pulled free from its clips. The blood on my haik. The sting on my face that will turn into a bruise. She looks at her haik, on the peg by the door, and leaves it there. She reaches back for her apron straps, and instead of untying it she re-ties the bow and straightens her shoulders before turning to open the door.

Mani is short, round, less than five-foot-tall, but she sweeps through the door into the alley as if she's Tin Hinan, the ancient Tuareg queen, coming to the rescue. Coming to the rescue. Standing up against the people attacking Ali. I watch and can barely breathe. What happens if they get her? What happens to everyone in the Palace of Birds? She is the glue of the place. When she dies the family will drift apart. Fall apart, like the palace. But now isn't the time to be gutless. Now is the time to walk behind her. To stand with her. To be brave. To pin my courage to the sticking place. Where the fuck is the sticking place anyway? I'd prefer to go back in the palace and look for somewhere to stick my courage, but Ali is brave, and I must be too. Big breath. Mani pushes past the crowd, hitting through the people surrounding Ali with what looks like a small baseball bat. Oh my God. She's got her zviti stick! The Naïlli stick that you use with a wooden bowl to mash up the orange spicey stuff that makes the most piss-awful meal you will ever taste (unless you like your taste buds being permanently rearranged). And it's still got zviti on it. So, she storms through to stand by Ali. And the men around her stand back, suck in their stomachs to move back, even if it's only an extra centimetre. Because they can hear their wives, 'What is this on your clothes? Eating on the street again, like a dog. Is my cooking not good enough? You think we have dinar to waste, when I've a family to feed?' Then Mani Aïcha really gets going.

'What is this? Why are you doing this to my boy, Ali? You think I fought the French to practise facing up to you one day? They had tanks, and mortars, and guillotines. They weren't a rabble. They were organised. Marching through these alleys. I remember you, Mohammed Haima. Licking your fingers after eating the sweets they threw at street rats. I remember you licking your fingers when I returned to the Casbah after bombing another café. And you, Salim? You've a pregnant wife. Only bad luck will come to you if you kill a man. If your baby is born dead, it will only be Allah exacting justice if you kill an innocent man.'

'He wasn't innocent. He was . . .'

'And don't get me started on you. You're Saïed's uncle. Have you so little confidence in your own flesh and blood that you think a good young man, a sweet young man, like Saïed, could do this abomination? Did you not watch him in the Mosque, his face closed to the world as he knelt? Go from here. Take Saïed's body to his mother, and you tell her what you have done. You tell her that you started rumours, and that her boy went so mad with the horror of what you said that he thought he could fly to Paradise? Take him. Take his body. Then come back with a bucket and soap and clean your crime from this alley. Before his mother sees it.'

She is systematic. She knows everyone. Remembers the details, the key that unlocks the bit that is full of shame, or the thing they are scared about, or the detail that they thought no one knew. She has watched them from the palace rooftop for fifty years.

The mob is easing back. At its edges the men are no longer mob, but audience. Wanting to go home.

Hoping to avoid Mani Aïcha's attention, but captured, wondering what she will say next. And here's the thing. You can punch a man who insults you. You can scream insults if the person you are screaming at can stand up to you but combined with the insults spewing from her mouth, they can see an old woman. An old woman who saw them sprawling naked on the birthing bed before she had put on their first nappy and passed them into their father's arms. An old woman who held them before their mothers had. And how do you argue with that? They see their Amti Aïcha, who always had a cup of squash and a biscuit for them on a hot day. And I love her too. I love her fierceness. The way she demands everything she wants from life. And I want to be just like her.

'Get back from my boy,' she says.

'He's not your boy. He's the baker's boy.'

And Mani inflates, she stands taller, raises her head, and comes to stand straight in front of the man who shouted; smearing the zviti stick against the centre of his chest.

'He is marrying my granddaughter. He is as much my boy as any of the men of my family.'

And that's the coup de grâce. The deathblow. The steam is released from the men standing in the alley. One of the women – yes there are women there too – puts a hand on my shoulder and begins to congratulate me, until she realises that because of her, and the men and Saïed's uncle, my so-called fiancé has been accused of being gay. But it's my turn to be brave. I had thought being brave was standing behind Mani Aïcha, but now I realise that being brave is to push forward, kneel carefully beside Ali, avoiding the bits of wood and stone and plaster that have been thrown at him, and lean forward over him, covering his battered face with my haik, opening my throat to release the ululating cry of an Algerian woman in anguish. I'm not good at it, but I'm good enough. They start to go home. They fall away, reversing from the centre of their attack. I watch them go. One by one. And I see Aïcha standing like the statue in Le Jardin du Hamma. She waits. They leave. The men start looking at each other, and then they put their hands in their pockets, and drop their shoulders, and start taking small individual steps away until when I look up a few minutes later I realise that Mani, Ali and I are alone; but as I sit back on my heels, I see Uncle Dahkman standing on the edge of the rooftop with an assault rifle. He puts his fingers to his lips, telling me not to tell Mani, and he steps back out of sight.

CHAPTER EIGHT

Ali is lying on his back, on the ground. I haven't had the courage to look yet. The courage to check if he is still breathing. I shut my eyes for a moment. Looking for the guts to open them again; but before I do, he groans. And my heart starts beating again.

'Mani, he's alive.'

'Stupid girl. Does he look dead?' Aïcha has seen dead bodies. She'd know.

'He's such a mess.'

'And if there is a mess, we tidy it. But before we tidy it, we need him inside.'

My Dad told me the hidden room was his secret. That only his dad, my grandfather, knew where it was. My dad had given me the secret, and I have owned it and kept it quiet. I don't want to tell Grandmother, but if ever we needed a hidden doorway from the alley, it is today.

'Mani, there's a room. Dad told me about it. There's a doorway . . .'

'Rabia, I know. I know everything about the palace. But your dad needed a secret. Every child needs a something that is just theirs, like you hide the photos of your mum at the bottom of your sewing box.'

Of course she would know. She watches everything. Listens behind every door. Right now, that's fine. I'll be pissed off about it tomorrow.

She's taken her apron off and rolled it into a thick strip that she's put under Ali's back, under his armpits. She grasps one end and passes the other end to me.

'They'll be back. Stop dreaming and move him.'

He's heavy. I try and pull him, kicking away some of the stones in our way. He's really heavy. I'm young and strong and healthy; but Mani is stronger than me. She leans back against the strap that she has wrapped round her wrists, and it is her weight that moves him. I try the same, but nothing happens. Nothing until Mani looks at me, shaking her head slightly.

'When I count. We can't do this unless we do this together.'

So we count. One, two – pull. One, two – pull. He moves about two inches. But then Uncle Dahkman is there, and my cousin Abu. And Dahkman pulls Ali backwards into his arms, with the tenderness of a man holding his firstborn, and Abu lifts his feet. Ali's face, under the dirt and mashed flesh turns pale. And then his face relaxes.

'He's . . .' I don't know how to finish the sentence. Can't talk, just point.

'He's fainted, Rabi. It's best he's fainted. This will hurt him less,' Dahkman says.

I walk ahead of Dahkman as he pauses for a

moment, before moving backwards to the twist of alley with its secret door. There isn't a secret catch that makes the wall spin silently out the way. The door is part of an illusion. There's a wall, and a narrow space, and if you go through the space there is a wooden door. It's the sort of thing you can't see until you see it, and then it is obvious. Like those images on Facebook that are a man and a horse and a vase, and you can see all three if you know what you're looking for; but until you do it's only the man, or only the horse, or only the vase. Until Dad showed me, this was only a wall. So Ali is carried through. Into the darkness with the stools and the table, and my box on the shelf. Mani pushes the cupboard that goes into my bedroom and drags the top mattress from the bed. It's made up of thin mattresses, like in the Princess and the Pea. I go behind Mani and pull one of the red blankets from the shelf. I move to put it on the mattress, but Dahkman and Abu are already putting Ali on the thin bed, breathing hard.

'How much pain au chocolat does this man eat?' Dahkman asks.

I'm sure I hear Mani snigger. But then she's all business.

'Rabia go and fetch a basin of hot water. Abu, go tell your maman to take the boys and sweep the street. She needs to sweep the little alley too, so that it all looks the same. After that go and sit on the roof. Watch everything. Warn us if they come back. Dahkman, secure the door from the alley, and go and fetch Amal to help her sister. And Rabia, you're going to wash the dirt off. Take pieces of an old sheet and cover his cuts once they're clean. Amal will bring candles. When he's clean Dahkman and Abu will change his clothes. You aren't to . . .'

I don't want to be told that I shouldn't look at his man bits, so I answer very quickly, 'Yes Mani . . . no.' I wish I didn't blush so easily.

And then Mani puts out a hand and touches my shoulder. 'I'm going to tell Ali's Mum that he's still breathing. I won't take long.'

Mani is wasted running a family. She should be running a country.

***

I don't know where to start. Amal has brought the warm water to me and is standing in the doorway. Her mouth is open, and she is staring at the hole behind the cupboard, and Ali lying on the floor covered in blood and dust. Time for me to be my grandmother's girl.

'Don't stand there like a goldfish. Bring the bowl here, and then you can start tearing up some towels, and one of the sheets.'

'I've got cotton wool,' Amal says, turning towards her backpack.

'Why?'

'To take my nail varnish off.' I'm caught between the 'of course you have, with your pretty little nails' and gratitude. I opt for gratitude.

'Thanks, Amal.'

We sit either side of Ali, on the floor. I take a small piece of cotton wool and wipe it near the cut that goes through his right eyebrow. He'd be blind if it was an inch lower. I'm about to wipe at it again when Amal puts her hand over mine.

'Only clean it once per cotton wool ball. Then throw the cotton wool away.'

'Where did you learn that?' Amal looks sheepish.

'I was a Girl Guide.' My hands keep doing, and I wash the scrapes and cuts. Gentle. Firm. Not wasting a single cotton wool ball. I catch myself on one of those laughs that you aren't supposed to laugh, when something is so absurd that you can't help yourself.

'What would Brown Owl say about this?' I ask.

We sit, stifling our giggles as we clean Ali's face, and the deep scrape on his neck, and get fresh water to rinse his hands. And I only stop giggling when I realise that most of the blood didn't come from Ali. And then I start crying. I don't stop until Mani Aïcha comes with a tray. More hot water, and two cups. There's coffee for Amal, and Mani has made me a cup of very English tea in the mug with the sweet peas. She pushes me out the way and takes over. Washing the blood from his hair.

***

I don't know what time it is. The doctor has been. I don't know how Mani persuaded him to come here, and I am not sure how she trusts him to keep quiet. I watched as he examined Ali's face. Put some careful stitches to bring the gashes on his face together. He apologised to Ali. Said that he hadn't any local anaesthetic. But he didn't look sorry. Said Ali wouldn't be quite such a pretty fellow now, would he? Pressed his cheek bones. I suppose he wanted to see if the bones of Ali's face were broken. Shone the light of a pen torch into his eyes. He checked his chest. Pressed hard against the bruises, until Mani kicked at the doctor's ankle.

'If you want paying, you'll stop hurting him.'

'I didn't hurt him, madame. He would take a lot to damage. He's tough. Got a skull made of concrete.' Ali opens his eyes. And says something very rude.

The doctor looks from Mani Aïcha to Ali. He reaches into his pocket and takes out a small bottle of pills. He passes it to me.

'Paracetamol. Oh great. Is that it?' I ask.

The doctor shrugs and walks past Mani, out the room.

Mani has put a jug of water on the table. I take a glass. Take the Paracetamol and put it to Ali's lips. Put my arm under Ali's shoulders and try not to hear the moan that comes from deep inside him. The movement of his lips reopens a cut, and I hold the hem of my blouse against his lip while he takes a very careful sip. Pour some drops of water onto the fabric and hold it there until the trickle of blood stops.

I'm the still place in the middle. Like one of those magic lantern things. I'm the candle and round the edge of the room shadows move, come and go. Bring me food that I don't want to eat. Bring me a blanket. Push me through the door into my room, and Amti Nassima undresses me like a child and changes me into fresh pyjamas. And she puts me into bed, and pulls the covers up round me. Tucks me in, like Mum used to. Then Nassima sits there, stroking my hair back from my face. Smoothing it back. She sits on the edge of the bed, holds my hand very still in hers. So, I shut my eyes, slow my breathing. I pretend to be asleep. And very quietly she leaves the room.

It's still dark outside when I hear him. Ali's making a deep heavy-breathed sobbing noise. As if it hurts to breathe. I get up. Pull a shawl round my shoulders, and I go to Ali. Sit beside him on the floor. I hold his hand, squeeze it very gently, and his sobbing slows, and he squeezes my hand back.

'Saïed. Is he . . .?'

'He's dead.' Maybe I should use some sort of euphemism. Passed away. Met his maker. Popped his clogs. I heard someone call death planting turnips with a stepladder. Never quite got that one. Took flight. Kicked the bucket. Gone to a better place. But I can't tell Ali any of those. Because sometimes it needs to be obvious. To be clear. So that's it. Short. Neat. Brutal. Telling Ali what he knows.

'I wanted it to be a dream.'

What do I say to that?

'Me too.'

I lay down next to him. My face against the top of his arm, because it will hurt to cuddle against him. I can't tuck myself under his arm, so I lie close to him, enjoying his warmth. I am so grateful that he's warm. That Mani was in time. That he didn't pop his clogs, kick the bucket, go to a better place. So grateful that he didn't fly to the angels with Saïed.

CHAPTER NINE

I'm not sure which call to prayer I can hear. It's like a fly walking on my skin. An irritant. I'd rather stay asleep. I notice things slowly. How warm I am. The blanket over me. Over us. The darkness of the hidden room. The sound of Mani Aïcha's slow breathing. She's sitting on a stool in the doorway. She smiles at me, her eyes wrinkling. I decide not to move.

'So, he's nice and warm then?'

'What do you mean?'

'You'll have to marry him now.' The laughter ripples up and through me. That hysterical laughter that can't be controlled.

'He's hardly had his wicked way with me, Mani!'

'Ah well. The bread will be cheap.' I sigh. And giggle. Shrug my shoulders and snuggle up to Ali's chest, making him wince. Because he survived them. Because he was rescued in time. Because it may not be storybook true love, but my world would have been wrecked, torn inside out, if he hadn't made it.

Amal and I take it in turns. We swap with the calls to prayer. Mani Aïcha takes the morning watch. From the call just before dawn. She arrives, carrying a clean towel, and a bowl of water. The first time she came I thought she was going to wash him, but then she started to carry out the ritual washing before prayer. Thorough, methodical, the hundred thousandth time. She washes as if there is nothing strange about washing her feet in a dark little room, built into the wall of a crumbling hareem. Then she kneels, and puffs through the motions of her prayers. Righteousness praying next to Ali, lying on his low mattress, bruised and beaten because he loved another man.

When she has finished praying, she stands, puts on her slippers, and rolls up the towel; before passing it to me. 'Put it with the washing, Rabia.'

I take it from her without any resentment. Something has shifted in our relationship. It's because I owe her something. She would probably say that I owe her everything. Taking over from Dad when my mum died. Giving me a roof. A family. Keeping my hands busy to stop me from dwelling on the miseries. But none of those things were ever wanted. I never thought of them as important, because I've been killing time. Waiting for Dad to come home, or to turn nineteen. I don't know why nineteen is the magic number of freedom and adulthood in Algeria. I won't need the paperwork signed by Dad when I'm nineteen. I'll be able to go home.

I go down to the kitchen to wash the bowl and find a fresh towel. Amti Nassima is waiting. There is a difference between sitting in the kitchen, just being there, and waiting. The difference is the tea in the sweet pea mug on the table, sitting next to a chocolate hobnob. Where on earth did she find those? So, what's the plan? What does she want to say? To tell me to do? There is always something that I must be told to do. I look at her, and wait, but she just sits there, next to me. Elbows on the table, sipping her own cup of very English tea. Mani buys French tea, but it is dark and bitter. Nassima gets English tea and today she has brought out the little silky sachets with real leaves inside.

'Are you wanting to tell me something?'

Nassima shakes her head, and leans over the cup, her hair loose and curling round the sides of the cup like a curtain. There's a little plop into the cup and a ring ripples out. She's crying. But then she does say something.

'It was yesterday that you were all children. You, following after Ali and Saïed as soon as you could toddle. Did I do something wrong? Could I have made a difference, maybe noticed something? Could I have prayed harder? Is it a punishment because I . . .?' and she pushes her cup towards me, and leans down on the table, her shoulders shaking with sobs.

'It's done, Naz. Saïed ended it all. We have to let it rest there and look after Ali now. If we talk about it, we waste what Saïed did. We can't even talk about it. We carry on as normal. Even if the normal is new.'

So we do normal. I do the washing, and wind the mangle, and put the sheets in the large tubs and take them onto the roof to dry. Nassima walks with the little ones to school. Amal pretends that she is lazy and

European and stays in her room until the sun is high; and then we sit together, and Amal passes me the school notebooks, and I read the story of the women we came from, which is right, because they'd get this, because they would sit with us in all of this.

CHAPTER TEN

Jamila didn't come back.

My mother became quieter and quieter in her waiting, pulling me onto her lap and wrapping a blanket round both of us. She waited beside the fire until the wood was ash. I know that she waited all night, because she kept me in her arms that night, like a younger child. Everyone else went back to the camp beyond the Medina, but my mother waited until the first piercing light of sunrise and then she carried me back to our camp in her arms before pushing me away and telling me to fetch our water and find fuel for the cooking pit. After baking flatbreads in the sand, she pulled me back into her arms, in the shade of our tent, and held me tightly, until the sun had risen halfway up the sky when she pushed me away again and told me to go and watch the dancers practising.

My mother went to the drummers and told them that Jamila hadn't returned. They smirked, and muttered to each other with wide grins, and my mother turned away, but then I noticed Abdulkader. He had been sitting under the edge of his tent filing the rough edges from a poured-silver pendant. He rose to his feet and approached my mother. He whispered something to her, and she half turned her back, putting her hand between them until he said something else. Turning to face him, she nodded. I watched as Abdulkader pulled his veil to cover his nose and mouth and taking his sword, he secured it in the scabbard that he had decorated with silver. He nodded once towards the men, who had stilled to watch him as he left our camp, going towards the place where the girls had danced.

I remember that day because my mother was angry. She smacked my hands when I was clumsy, pushing the couscous too close to the edge of the bowl so that some of the grains landed on the ground, and she shouted at me when I dropped pomegranate seeds on my dress, staining it red. Hayat came and sat with us to eat, but she left quickly, removing herself from the biting circumference of my mother's anxiety. Everyone was quiet, and that day lasted longer than any other day, but suddenly, just as the sun touched the horizon, the camp started to breathe again as we saw a man wearing a blue shesh at the edge of our camp. Abdulkader had returned. As he got closer, we realised that he carried Jamila, silent in his arms, covered by his long robe. He was breathless when he reached our campfire. His face was drawn, and the boy who had carried me on his shoulders the day before had gone, replaced by a serious man. He went straight into our tent, indicating with his head that my mother should follow.

I crept after them, looking under the edge of the tent

where the ropes are tied. My mother and Hayat took Jamila, and I heard my mother as she began to cry. Fear knifed into me, that only lessened when I heard my sister's voice, very quiet, in the dusk. Two of the other women boiled water, and found soft cloths, like they bring when a baby is being born. I didn't understand because, of course, there was no baby. I heard sobbing from inside the tent and saw the bowls of water being brought back out. It was still light enough to see that the sand where the water was poured had turned red.

Abdulkader had left the tent by then, and he took his turban, and dampening the end of it he took his sword and started cleaning the blade. When he had finished, he screwed up his shesh, his beautiful indigo veil, and threw it into the fire where the oily dye caught quickly and turned the flames themselves blue.

That night we did something very strange. We broke camp before dawn, and we left. We normally broke camp in daylight, but everyone was in a hurry. We had no camel of our own, but our tent was strapped to the singer's camel, and we carried our other belongings on our backs. Abdulkader carried Jamila.

I had seen Jamila's face by then. She was covered in bruises. Her fingers were swollen, and her nails broken. Sometimes she cried out as we crossed the uneven ground towards our mountains, and my mother would find a small blue bottle containing a sticky brown liquid and press a little into Jamila's mouth before we continued our journey. Abdulkader was a silversmith, but he had first been a blacksmith and hours of pounding metal had given his shoulders breadth and strength. He carried my sister as if she weighed nothing, but as if she was the heaviest burden in the world. It took us two days, moving fast, before we arrived at the village we came from.

It should have been better to be home, but the others kept their distance from us – from my mother, and Jamila. Hayat went back to her own mother's tent and the men gathered round Abdulkader whispering but growing silent if I went too close. It was then that I learnt something. When something very bad or very wrong or very important is happening, children are not noticed if they are quiet and still. I was quiet and still as I watched Abdulkader go to my sister. He took a piece of leather that had been bundled with string and tucked into the front of his robe. She opened it and shuddered. It was full of silver coins.

'It's your money. I took everything those bastards carried and sold it all. This is your money.'

My mother looked anxiously at the money in Jamila's hands, but she didn't argue. She looked as if she wanted to, but she kept her mouth shut.

'What do you want me to make for you?' Abdulkader asked Jamila.

Jamila pushed the coins back at Abdulkader.

'I want bracelets. The most beautiful, fiercest bracelets you have ever made.'

Abdulkader worked late into the night, and by morning he had melted down the silver and coins, and my sister had the spiked bracelets of a Naïlliyat dancer.

Abdulkader started to gather his belongings after that, and was preparing to leave, but we saw the sky above the sand moving in the distance, showing us that we had visitors.

In the desert you know that something is happening, someone is coming, when the haze above the sands is disturbed by movement. We watched for several hours as the haze turned into a smudge, and a low distant noise. The small marks grew, and a thrill of excitement passed through the people watching with me.

The people travelling across the sands towards us were carried on the backs of camels, and were distinct because they, like Abdulkader, wore beautiful indigo cotton veils wrapped as turbans and pulled down across their mouths, so that only their noses and eyes showed. The sunlight shone bright on their silver crosses, making them white against the deep blue of their clothing. As they grew closer, I could see their daggers sheathed in silver scabbards. They were Tuareg tribesmen.

Abdulkader stood in the doorway of our family tent watching as they approached, his hand shading his eyes against the brightness of the desert. He too wore a long necklace but his carried several crosses. They were a sign that he was accepted by different tribes and was kin to many families. Each cross represented a different group. What was missing that day was his shesh. His head was bare, and his black hair reached his shoulders in soft curls and waves. It should have been a woman's hair.

When the Tuareg reached the centre of the camp their camels dropped, obedient, to their bellies allowing their riders to dismount. One of the men bore himself differently from the others. His robes were more elaborate, and he wore silver rings on the joints of each finger. He stood, surrounded by his men, looking for something. When his eyes settled on Abdulkader it was obvious that he had found what he was looking for. His face, deep-lined by dust from the desert, broke into a smile of an all-encompassing happiness. He leapt forwards and held Abdulkader by his shoulders for a moment before drawing him into his arms.

I didn't speak their language then. I didn't understand what was being said. What I saw was a father ruffling the long, uncovered hair of a beloved son, and calling out to one of his men who brought a long piece of deep blue cotton to wrap around his son's head and across his face. I brought them bowls of water from our well, and the men took the bowls with them into the shade of the tents.

Abdulkader sat for several hours talking quietly while his father listened. Perhaps he talked about his travels. Maybe he talked about the beautiful silver jewellery that he had made. More likely he told his father about the crime he had committed, and the courage required. More likely he told his father about a little Naïlliyat dancing girl of whom he was fond. He rested his covered head against his father's shoulder as he talked and talked.

The Tuareg stayed with us that night. They slept in their own tents, constructed from mats and ropes, but first they sat by the fire and watched the dancing girls. It was strange to watch the Tuareg because they didn't stand to dance but sat with their arms moving above their heads in time to the music and the movements of the girls they watched. Later they told stories of a Berber queen, Tin Hinan, buried in a large desert fortress and of Barbary pirates and djinn with flying carpets. Abdulkader told me that while outsiders believe the Tuareg tie their mats with ropes to make tents, it is really to stop the rugs and carpets flying off into the night.

I slept well that night with my head full of stories and magic.

When morning came, I was woken by Abdulkader whispering to my mother in the corner of our tent. He told her what he had been told by his father. Three French soldiers had been found several miles from the oasis of Bou Saâda. Their hands had been bound, and their feet had been cut off. They had been left to bleed to death, and anything of value had been taken from them. The people of Bou Saâda had heard screaming, and a policeman from the French town had seen a lone Tuareg coming from the place where the bodies were found. The Tuareg had carried a girl, and his robes had been spattered with the stains from arcs of bright blood.

Our mother started packing all she had of the dry couscous, flatbreads and strips of smoked meat. She brought out her beautiful pearls and wrapped them in a square of blue-white silk before handing them to Abdulkader. I watched as Jamila came to the doorway of our tent, steadying herself by leaning on a long piece of wood that I had collected for our fire. She had been so joyful, but her eyes were tired and shadowed now, and the flesh below her eyes was pale. She was carrying a bundle containing all her possessions and a smaller bundle that held mine.

Our mother turned to me, 'You and Jamila are going to visit Abdulkader's family. It will be safer for you there. Abdulkader can't travel alone now, and he needs to go back to his people; and we think that you and your sister will be safest away from here, travelling with him.'

A child doesn't ask how long she will be gone if the adventure before her includes camels, a beloved sister, and nights around desert campfires with nomadic travellers who carry with them all the ancient stories. I kissed my mother's cheek, so anxious to be gone that my breath barely fell upon her face.

I was only little and given the honour of riding the same camel as Abdulkader's father. Abdulkader carried Jamila on his camel, wrapped against the dust and dirt of the desert in the new lamb's wool cloak given him by his father.

I've told you before that if you are always travelling that all journeys are the same and that destinations become less important; but to a child the journey south lasted its own lifetime. We passed dry riverbeds, and the high mountains of the Hautes Plaines were soon behind us. We travelled across scrublands and circled the vast salt plains where a man who doesn't know, or isn't careful, can sink through the crust of salt and be swallowed by the brown liquid mess beneath.

We rarely saw anyone else, and sometimes it felt as if the desert would never end, and that we were lost like the Jewish people who had been confused by their God for forty years; but these men knew the stars and the path of the sun and the routes that passed through the oases.

I soon learnt why the men wore their indigo cotton across their faces. The oily dye caught the dust. The sand was everywhere. In our hair, and our eyes and mouth. It spread through every article we carried and was the grit in every mouthful of stew and bite of bread.

When the sandstorms came, rising like a wall, the Tuareg formed a circle, sheltered against their camels, each covering their face with their shesh until the storm passed over like the Angel of Death, high-pitched, bitter and relentless. Abdulkader and his father each took their shesh and covered our faces until the storm passed. After the storm our faces were tinged blue, like corpses, from the indigo. Maybe that is why the Angel of Death didn't stop with the Tuareg and steal our souls away. Perhaps our blue skin tricked him.

I don't know how long the journey lasted. In the desert the days pass with the rise and fall of the sun and the waxing, waning moons. You measure time with the growth of a woman's belly or in waiting for the birthing of a favourite camel; and finally, with the changing landscapes. As we reached the south the land gradually became greener and more fertile. Streams replaced the dried-up riverbeds, and we saw more people. Sometimes the Tuareg would go to a town where they were well-known, to trade in silver, amber or smooth agate stones. There seemed no end to the journey. At each settlement I thought, 'ah, we are home now', and then we left each settlement; but there came a day when we arrived.

We reached a green valley, with a clear river running through, fed by a spring. It was here that Abdulkader urged his camel into a loping run, rushing ahead of everyone else, and as he reached a small structure built from the sand and mud of the riverbed his camel went to its knees without being told and Abdulkader slid down and picking up the hems of his robe he ran like a child to the doorway of the hut and flung himself, like the boy he had been so recently, into the arms of a small dark-skinned woman who welcomed him. The boy become a man. The beat of her heart. We were all welcomed by Abdulkader's mother, Sayeeda.

I replace the notebook on the shelf, reaching for the next, but Mani shakes her head, and points at Ali. He is sleeping. His face peaceful. I leave the cahier on its pile, and then, ignoring Grandmother I lie down on the floor next to Ali, watching his face as he sleeps.

It's a kind of declaration. Lying here next to Ali. The decision to lie down. Amal looks from me to Grandmother and back again. Not sure what she's watching but knowing that it matters.

Grandmother smiles at me. 'So, you've decided.'

'Yes.'

Amal looks from me to Grandmother. Back again. 'Decided what?'

'I'm going to marry him.'

Amal's shoulders drop.

'Please don't.'

'I don't think I have a choice.'

'If you don't have a choice now, you'll end up with harder choices later. When you've kids. When everyone has settled into all his lies and excuses. It will drag things up then. For goodness' sake, Rabia. Wait for something worth your dress.'

'You mean love, I suppose. I read about it all the time, but it doesn't happen. Not really. I could wait forever and end up like Amti Fatima. Alone, watching other peoples' families grow up. I can't not marry him. They'll come back if I don't. You saw what they did. I have to marry him.'

'He shouldn't ask you to. You might as well be his sister. He should not be asking you.'

'You haven't been here long enough. This disgrace. This shame. I don't want him alone in it. I don't want his mum unable to go to the souk because of the other women whispering into their haiks each time she walks past.'

'But it isn't your fault. You aren't to blame.'

'Do you think Ali is to blame? A heart chooses what it chooses. He didn't wake up one day and decide to destroy everything he touches. He just loved Saïed. And I'm not stupid. If Ali was straight, he would never have wanted me. And if my mother hadn't died, I wouldn't be here, in the middle of this; but he did, and she did and I'm here. She was always worried about me coming to Algiers. She'd never visit because she thought she'd get trapped, but now she's gone it's me stuck here instead. She didn't want this for me, but I don't mind it as much as I thought I would.'

'Then you should. If you won't care, I will. Don't do what I did.'

I have tried to resist asking questions. I want to interrogate her. Maybe it's time, but I won't have this conversation with someone who's going away.

'You're going to leave again, aren't you?' She comes to sit on the floor beside where I'm lying and puts out a hand to stroke my hair. I almost pull back, but then I don't, and she starts to curl a strand of my hair round her fingers.

'Yes. I'll leave. But not yet.'

'Thought so. Everyone leaves. Mum, Dad, and you'll go too. I don't think I want to know what you did. I don't want to start knowing you because I–'

'We'll keep in touch though. I'll keep in touch.'

'Are you keeping in touch with whoever you ran away from?'

'No.'

'Well then.' But she still takes another strand of hair, curling it.

'Why did you leave them?'

She hesitates.

'I didn't leave a "them". I left a "him".'

What do I say to that?

'Why?'

'Oh, Rabia. There aren't enough exercise books in the world to explain that.'

'Did he hurt you?'

'Not with his fists, but there's more than one way to hurt. I wanted to get away, and think, and decide whether to go back or not.'

I'm still lying on the floor but roll away from Ali to face my sister. And she lies down in the dust of the floor, facing me.

'So I won't leave. Not really. Because I don't have anyone to go back to.'

'You have us. You have Mani, Amti Nassima, Uncle Dahkman, the cousins . . .'

'It's not the same.'

Something pulls inside of me at that. Because I get it. I'm hooked. She'll leave. In spite of what she says, she'll go. She won't be here, and I will spend forever missing her. Because, so far as sisters go, in my limited experience, Amal is alright.

The world closes in. The trap is the same. It's still

here, in the Palace of Birds, but it is as if I'm getting smaller, my needs subsumed. As if I am a mouse in a bowl, and the bowl is growing around me, making it more and more impossible to climb up the sides and get out.

'Will you tell me about this "him" some time?'

'If you tell me about Mokhi, your dad.'

A mouse in a bowl. Smaller and smaller.

There's a parcel when I go to bed. Tissue paper wrapped in pink ribbon, like they have in the boutique in the hotel. And inside there is hand cream, really posh hand cream, a manicure set with a glass nail file, and nail varnish. I wrap them back up, not wanting to look at them, but I hold the parcel against me, stroking the satin of the ribbon as I fall asleep.

CHAPTER ELEVEN

Ali's mother has come to see him. Of course she has. I hadn't planned her visit in my head. Hadn't expected to see her at all, being so busy with Ali, and the thought of Saïed falling fills my days, except in the moment I wake, before remembering.

I've always got on okay with her. Known her since I was a child in London. But she's not English. She didn't spend time with anyone English. Not even my mum. She thought Mum was too racy. Maybe not that word. Not modest. Not righteous. She didn't approve of Mum because Mum didn't behave like an Algerian girl. Well, she wouldn't have, would she? She was a young woman living by herself in London until she met Dad. And she lived with him with nothing more than a ring on her finger. Well, that's how she put it. No marriage certificate. No vows. No party. Just the words, and a couple of witnesses. Nothing with proof. It bothered her. And the women, like Ali's mum, never quite knew what to make of her. But they liked me.

They saw me as a little soul to cosset and teach. Ali's Mum had me cooking in her kitchen in Finsbury Park before I went to primary school. Ali would sit at the table doing his homework for Saturday school, and I'd be trying to make pastries or bread. Sometimes he'd give me advice, quietly, in English.

'A smidge more flour.'

'Wash your hands in cold water. You'll melt the butter.'

'If you use the salted butter, it will taste better.'

My baking was always better when Ali was in the kitchen watching. His mum would ask what he said, and I'd reply, 'He's asking when I'm going home, going to be finished, going to get it right.'

So it's a shock when she doesn't say, 'Saha, Rabia.' Hello. She won't look at me. Doesn't give me a hug. I leave her to it and come up to sit on the roof. Miriam, Ali's Mum, follows me.

'You'll marry him then?' Mani Aïcha has followed us up. I look from Aïcha to Miriam and back. They're waiting.

I've done a pros and cons list in one of my cahiers.

Pro: I like him.

Pro: he's my friend.

If I don't, I'll make a liar out of Grandmother.

If I don't, Ali doesn't have a nice little bride as an alibi, an Ali Bye. Oh shit.

If I don't marry him, the men will come back.

If we aren't planning a wedding . . .

Con: I'm not in love with him.

Con: If I marry him, I will never fall in love. Find out how it feels.

But the plus is that if we get married, I get to go home to England.

I'm beyond choosing. I look at Grandmother and nod. She nods back. A tiny movement. Miriam purses her lips.

'You should have agreed sooner. Boys don't turn to other boys if they've a warm girl in their bed at night. You should have got married two years ago. When we first said.'

'I'm eighteen. I was only sixteen then.'

'And what has that to do with me? You'd have a baby on your lap and have learnt to be a wife by now. If you'd just married him Saïed wouldn't be dead.'

Anger rises in me. Bubbles up. Spills over at the unfairness. 'I wasn't caught in bed with Saïed, was I?'

The slap, hard on my face, surprises me, and tears rise, following and flowing into the anger spilling upwards.

'No. And there's the pity of it. You'd have saved all of us this shame.'

'And be shamed instead?'

'You're marrying him anyway.' I open my mouth and shut it and open it again. Grandmother puts her hand on my sleeve, pinching my arm.

'Downstairs. Now.' So I leave them. The sunshine and fresh air on the terrace has gone stale. I go downstairs, take my scarf, and head to the door. Then I see Amal has followed me and is pulling another scarf from the hook. She walks with me, as if I had invited her.

'What's happened? What did she want with you?'

'She wanted to tell me that everything is my fault

because I should have agreed to marry Ali sooner.'

'Agreed? So you've done it then. You said yes to them. Everyone will know now.'

'Yes.'

She takes a quick step, gets in front of me, stops me moving forward.

'They can't make you,' she says. As if it is simple.

'They don't need to. I have no choice. Grandmother has told everyone. She will look stupid if I don't. Ali might be attacked again. What choice do I have?'

'Let Ali worry about that.' She doesn't understand. She doesn't understand family and honour and that we do what we have to when we are loving our families.

'I can't just leave him now.'

'You can. If I left my husband, then you can leave Ali.' I feel everything cloying the air around me. Getting up my nose and into my lungs so fast that I don't want to breathe, and in this moment not breathing would surely be a blessing. There is too much happening, and I don't dare ask Amal what she's talking about because I can only cope with the bits I can cope with. And the bits I can cope with don't include her.

When we get back Miriam has gone. Aïcha is sitting on the bed in my room. She doesn't say a thing when I walk back into the room with Amal. She just picks up her sewing, and leaves. Maybe she's feeling guilty. Or maybe she's just pissed off.

Amal goes to the shelf and picks up the next cahier and passes it to me.

'I don't think I can bear to think about any of this right now. Will you read to us?'

I turn to the next page of Jamila's story and start to read it aloud.

CHAPTER TWELVE

In the years that followed Sayeeda was our foster mother, and she loved me as I loved her; but she held back from Jamila. I think it was because she recognised the danger in Jamila; that she had brought her son close to destruction and might do so again.

Jamila hated being dressed as a Tuareg. Sayeeda, Abdulkader's Mother, set about hiding our appearance with enthusiasm. She pulled Jamila's hair into smooth waves using a rough wooden comb, and then dividing it into small sections plaited it into long plaits that reached her waist. Jamila winced and fidgeted, full of stiff-backed objections. We went unveiled, as in our own place and tribe, and our clothing was plain and less elaborate, but Jamila missed the pretty dancing dresses and layered embroidery of the Ouled Naïll. Abdulkader's mother would look at our small blue tattoos, and she would cover our faces with henna paste or walnut oil to hide them and paint small black lines over them before smearing red paste across our foreheads and cheeks.

The more we looked like the Tuareg the less danger we would bring.

Jamila slowly healed, and we settled into life with the Tuareg, but while I enjoyed learning to work leather into the belts, pouches and bridles that we traded, she would sit staring at nothing, her hands idle, watching for Abdulkader until Sayeeda would speak sharply and pull her back to her task. When the day's work was done, I would go to watch Abdulkader. The other blacksmiths tried to shoo me away, so I remembered to sit quietly, watching from a distance, and sometimes for my patience I was allowed to go closer to watch as Abdulkader melted silver and copper together to pour into sand moulds. Then he would give me a small file, and we would sit together bringing the fine marks of the silver to life.

Jamila asked what he was making in those quiet evenings. He smiled at her and told her they were bride gifts, and one day he would give them to . . . he paused. One day he would give them to the girl who had his heart. My sister went back to the leather, but her hands slipped frequently until Sayeeda told her to go and fetch water, or cook, or tidy or do anything, but please do anything somewhere else, where Sayeeda wouldn't have to watch her sulks.

We were accepted by the people in that camp, but never as part of them. We would sit round fires, like the Ouled Naïll, and the blacksmiths would tell stories. I learnt to dance with my hands, and I learnt all the songs and stories by heart. Jamila was too busy watching Abdulkader from beneath the veil of her plaited hair to listen to the stories, but she too learned to speak, talk, *work and look like a Tuareg woman.*

A Naïlli girl who can dance, and who has her moon times, is a woman in our tribe, but somehow Abdulkader never seemed to see Jamila as a woman. That would have been bearable to my sister, but Abdulkader noticed, smiled and flirted with every woman except her. She could see no one but him, but he smiled and talked to the other girls, and when she saw his camel grazing outside a woman's tent at night, she would lower her eyes in anger. I had the freedom of childhood to spend time with Abdulkader, but he never seemed to see or acknowledge her.

He took lovers but, like the other unmarried men, nothing was ever said so long as they went to their women after dark and left before dawn. Jamila would rise early and find reasons to sit in the opening of the tents, watching to see where he went and with whom. If she had waited, he would have seen her. He would have noticed her. I wonder now if he held back because he had noticed her. I know that he would never have noticed me.

I remember the evening that Jamila ruined everything. I was sitting, resting my head on my foster mother's shoulder. We had eaten after a busy day spent preparing for the camel races but hadn't noticed that Jamila wasn't there. We didn't notice until she arrived, dressed in the thick-layered robes of a Naïlliyat. Her head and shoulders were covered in coins, and round her neck she wore our mother's pearls. She carried the white-blue veil of a dancer and wore the spiked defensive bracelets Abdulkader had made. She was exquisite.

When Jamila had danced at Bou Saâda she had been joy and life but now she danced with a subtle hunger, her eyes only on one man. The years had turned her into a woman and as she started to dance, arms high and extended, moving under the veil, she sang a love song that only we understood. It was the song of a girl waiting beneath the harvest moon for a lover who never came. The men were fascinated by everything she did. Her beauty, her costume, her song, her dance. Abdulkader had never looked sadder or more serious.

When Jamila finished dancing, her skin shining, and her breath rapid and shallow she looked up and saw our foster mother's face. Our foster mother pushed me away and, grabbing Jamila by the back of her hair, pulled her from the campfire. The screaming and shouting and crying went on until dawn. In the morning Abdulkader's mother bundled our belongings into two leather bags and shoved them at her son.

'You brought them here. You take them away. There is a caravan moving north two villages from here. Take them away before they curse us all. Go sell them to the slavers going to Algiers.'

That is how it happened that five harvests after leaving Bou Saâda we picked up our bundles and followed Abdulkader. We followed terrified. In the next village he exchanged three swords, his bride price silver and our pearls for three camels and provisions for the long journey home.

If you have ever spent six months on a camel crossing the Great Sands, you will know what it is to be patient. At first, we sang Naïlli songs to each other but as the desert stretched before us, we sacrificed Jamila's

99

dancing veil. Tearing it in half, we covered our mouths and noses with the blue-white silk. We learnt to be quiet under the stars as we travelled.

During the day we built a rope and mat canopy for shelter, and we obeyed Abdulkader when he told us how many mouthfuls of water we could drink. It was dangerous to travel in such a small group with the slave caravan so nearby, and Abdulkader worked hard to find secluded and sheltered camps. We travelled every night without rest. After three months we wandered, tired and dirty, into an oasis and the slaver from the south was there. He offered to buy us from Abdulkader in exchange for an extra four camels, so that Abdulkader could trade for himself with the north, but when Abdulkader refused, he spat on the ground and walked away.

When Abdulkader saw them in the distance a few days later, he made camp, and he made us wait for three days, even though we were running out of water. He told us that there are worse things than dying of thirst, and if we became part of the slave caravan, we would learn about them all.

I will never forget the moment that we realised that the oasis in the distance was Bou Saâda and saw the red and black striped tents of the Ouled Naïll pitched on the outskirts of the town. The camels, encouraged by our happiness lolloped and hurried forward. By the time we reached the tents everyone had stopped what they were doing to see who the visitors were.

My first question was to ask for my mother. Having seen the tents, I had expected to see her waiting, her arms outstretched and her face running with joyful tears. The man I had asked looked up at the three of us, still perched high on our camels.

'Zohra went back to the mountains. You should go to her there. The French soldiers were here, and they took our girls and young women. You won't be safe here. Especially not her.' He pointed at Jamila.

The soldiers, hearing that our girls were Naïlli had issued them with identity cards, identifying them as prostitutes, and taken them to the Bordel Mobile de Campagne. The travelling whore camp that serviced the soldiers.

So we began another journey. We stayed long enough to trade before continuing the long journey to the mountains; gathering supplies of water, food, and some of the spices and oils that I had learnt about in the south. It was cooler in the north, and it felt good to travel during the day. It meant that we could see the flat-topped mountains that were our destination.

When I was a child the mountain people had come running to meet strangers, full of curiosity; but no one came to meet us, looking for friends, or asking after relatives. The village was quiet. No one came out of the caves to greet us. Not even the children. We sat on our camels waiting, and it was several minutes before I saw a child being pulled back into the mouth of a tent. I told the camel to lie down, and I slid from its back. I stood watching and looked carefully at the tents until I found one that I recognised. There was something about its patterns, and the black and red stripes of camel hair. I went to the entrance of the tent. The smell was purulent and seared into me. Holding my breath I entered, gazing around in the dim light. It was the smell of sickness. A woman lay in the corner, on a thick pile of rugs.

I had learnt not to be afraid of sickness or death, accepting them as part of life's fullness. I had been taught that they were as important as love and the blessings of new life. I went to kneel beside the woman and greeted her. 'Saha.'

The woman opened her eyes and pushed herself up on one elbow, painfully, slowly. There was something about her eyes.

'Do I remember you?' I asked.

She smiled at me and then I saw it, the same smile as Jamila. The eyes like mine.

'Don't you remember me, Fatima? Is it that long?'

I felt a horror rise inside me. My mother had grown old. How could my beautiful mother grow old in five short years?

'What happened?' I asked.

'The soldiers came. I tried to make them take me instead of one of the younger girls, but they laughed, and pushed me away. When I carried on begging to be taken, they got annoyed, and one of them whipped my feet and legs with a belt to stop me from walking after them.' She raised her blanket, wincing as the wool pulled at her where the fibres had dried in her wounds. The smell of infection rose in my face, as I looked at the long thin wounds covered in thick yellow scabs that oozed puss. There were dark green, yellow and blue bruises up to her knees.

I had learnt a little about healing from my foster mother, and I raised the edges of the tent to let air pass through and took the dirty blanket to burn. I found fresh water, and boiled cloths before drying them in the sun and then taking herbs I made a paste with scented oils and a little of the frankincense oil I had recently bought, and slowly and meticulously set about cleaning my mother's legs, wrapping them in ointment and clean bandages. I bathed her arms and back with cool water to lower her heat, leaving the water on her skin so that the wind would blow away the heat with the moisture.

It felt wrong to be trying to heal her, because I had never walked with Death in his darkness before. The Tuareg believe that you must be close to death before you can tend the sick, because if you have chased death away for yourself you will know how to chase him away from others.

Jamila should have been our healer, but she wasn't interested. The smell offended her, and the sight of our mother's sickness and infected wounds brought her to tears. She wasn't interested in helping and disliked the closeness of our mother's tent.

While I was working and bathing my mother's face and arms the other women started to return. My aunts and cousins came and sat in the tent that now smelt of rose, frankincense and sweet healing oils, watching me and asking questions. They wanted to know about our travels, about Jamila's escape, about our time in the south. I looked for my friends, and girls my own age, but I saw none of them. After what my mother had said I didn't ask where they were.

It was later, once the work was done, that Jamila came back to the tent. The women fussed over her. Perhaps because they remembered her better. She was less strange, and she was old enough to remember what it was to be part of the Ouled Naïl. I had been a child when we left, and I still wore my hair like a Tuareg, wearing indigo robes. Jamila had washed her face on the journey across the desert and had worn the blue-white veils of a Naïlli dancer to protect herself from the sand, longing to become the girl she had been when she danced at Bou Saâda. She had already found a blouse and bodice to wear over a long skirt and looked like a Naïlliyat once more.

Life returned to whatever normal can be with so many people gone and missing. I continued to nurse my mother, and within a few weeks her legs, although still covered in lines and scars, could hold her weight and she began to leave the tent and help me make the flatbreads on low fires.

I had not noticed at first that the men I remembered from my childhood were missing. I asked my mother where they had gone.

'They are following the Bordel Mobile de Campagne. They keep their distance from the camp, but if any of our girls escape, or if the girls become too ill to carry on, they will be there to bring them home.'

Abdulkader and Jamila began to spend more time together, and she would sit and watch the working of the silver, making little suggestions and commenting on the things that she found beautiful. I was no longer welcome there, and stopped helping with the silver, even though there were no other men to disapprove, but my mother told me that it was time for me to leave the two of them alone.

It was a matter of weeks before the precious silver had been finished, and Jamila was given her treasure. There were celebrations, and Abdulkader moved into our family tent.

CHAPTER THIRTEEN

Jamila was flushed with happiness in those first weeks after her marriage. She had a sway to her steps and was smiling and happy. She reminded me of the joyful child who had first gone to Bou Saâda. She was less irritable with me and made no complaint if I sat near Abdulkader while he worked his furnace and made his jewellery. I was given beautiful white silver to work. The pure silver was soft and malleable and easier to decorate, but part of me loved the shine of the silver copper alloys. They reminded me of the moon when it glows warm above a desert sky. I worked small triangles into the silver, loving that they represented the women of my tribe and family. Each triangle a person. And I would use our ancient letters to hide words in the patterns. I think that when something is made – anything that is beautiful – that a part of its creator's soul is captured and carried in it. The emotions that it carries then affect the wearer. I used to imagine that the pearls my mother wore, traded weeks before for Abdulkader's camels, had carried with them the breath of the ocean where they were born. As I decorated the silver bracelets, I hoped for happiness for the women that wore them, and long life, and the safe bearing of children. I told Jamila that I wove hope into my patterns, and she laughed at me. She tapped my cheek and called me foolish.

It was a time without much silver for our tribe. There was a drought, and the women needed to sell their bracelets and coins. The crops failed, and the kids and lambs born to our flocks were smaller and there were fewer twins than in earlier years. The only steady income came from the tribesmen in the hills who would come down to the oasis after sunset looking for Abdulkader the Swordsmith. He had a reputation for fine work, and the long straight swords were clean and unblemished, forged using iron and coal.

Jamila grew impatient when the tribesmen came and would complain after they left. She couldn't understand why Abdulkader would risk so much by making their swords, but she never complained that her headdress was becoming heavy with small silver coins, or that her bracelets and rings were becoming more elaborate.

It was the next spring before I noticed that Jamila's swaying steps were becoming more laboured. The clothes of a Naïlliyat fall from below the breast, and Jamila's pregnancy wasn't apparent for several months. She took to sleeping in the afternoon, and drinking the herbal teas made by our mother. In the evening Abdulkader would take her for walks and for a season he stopped meeting with the tribesmen. I would watch them from the ropes of our tent, wondering what they talked about. I wondered what it is that makes a man *love a woman, and a woman love a man. I wondered how it was that I could love a man who only saw me as a little sister. How no one could see me clearly enough to realise what was in my heart.*

On the day the world changed the camp was unnaturally silent. We hadn't realised that the outside world was coming closer, but one day it arrived with all the power and vengeance and spite of a swarm of locusts. It left nothing behind.

I could hear the camels hobbled near the tents with their strange laugh-like brays, and the sheep and goats bleating and baaing to their young. The swallows were still dancing high in the sky, but the men and women of our tribe walked quietly, looking at the ground. I realised that they knew something I didn't.

I found one of my small cousins and a ball and started playing with him. I threw the ball into the ropes of the tents, and as I bent to pick up the ball, I listened carefully for any snippets of conversation. When I was near the tent of Hayat's mother, I heard something unexpected. I heard Hayat's voice. Hayat had been taken with the other girls to the Bordel Mobile de Campagne. I wasn't foolish enough to rush into the tent and demand if it was Hayat that I had heard, but I decided to go near the family tents belonging to other girls who had been taken. I gradually realised that four of our girls had returned in the night. Having gathered this information, and being fairly sure that I was correct, I went to find my mother.

My mother was baking thin loaves of bread on the metal tray above the fire. She turned the bread, sliding it between her hands before flipping it so that it didn't burn. I know she knew that I had arrived, because her shoulders tensed, but she didn't look up. I had learnt some childish wisdom around the Tuareg fires and went to sit close to her. I tapped her leg and looked up into her face.

'Hayat? Zarah? Lilia? Ayesha? Are they all back?'

My mother stopped concentrating on the fire and looked at me. 'You know nothing, little Fatima. Absolutely nothing. And if anyone asks anything you shall tell them that you know absolutely nothing.'

I nodded, but still had to ask, 'Are they all back?'

My mother nodded slightly and sighed as she turned the bread again.

'How?' I asked.

'Our men couldn't bear hearing them crying, and they went last night and took them. They tried to make it look as if the girls had escaped by themselves. The girls will be gone by tomorrow. The men will take them tonight, with the camels, and they will go away. That is all I am going to tell you, and if the soldiers come and threaten to rip out your tongue and cut off your ears you are to tell them forever that you know nothing.'

I stayed close to my mother for the rest of the day. We were all scared of the soldiers.

***

It was dark when my mother woke me. She had my blanket, a bundle with food and a leather purse with silver inside.

'You are to go to the mountains tonight. Go with your sister and Abdulkader. When the soldiers come, they will *be looking for four girls. They won't care if they recognise you, or if you are one of the missing girls. They will take you anyway. You need to go to the mountains with the others.'*

Travelling through the barren scrubland at night would have been difficult without the camels. I put my blanket across my camel's back and held tight to her soft white wool as she swayed to her feet.

We waited until the others were ready. Abdulkader had four camels. Even though it made him slower he carried Jamila on his camel, and the other camels carried Hayat and the others. My cousin came with her sisters, and another family that I didn't know sent their beloved daughters with us.

Abdulkader had learnt the skills of a Tuareg travelling in the camel trains with his father, and he was careful to keep us out of the moonlight, following the riverbeds and shadows. It was almost dawn when we arrived in the mountains and our tribe was expecting us. They took the girls, my sister and me into a cave, and there we hid.

The cave was cool during the day, but at night moisture collected on the inner walls chilling us. We were used to the busyness of all the women's tasks, but the enforced idleness unsettled us, and the darkness meant that we couldn't spin the camel hair and wool or sew and mend. We sat talking quietly, and only at dawn did we leave the caves for a few minutes, stretching our damp blankets on the ground to dry. We wondered what would happen to us and prayed to whatever gods chose to listen. Our prayers were simple. We wanted to survive.

The girls who had been rescued sat together, away from us. My sister would ask what had happened in the Bordel; but even though she was a married woman they guarded her innocence and mine, telling us nothing.

During the night the girls cried out in their sleep, and when Hayat started to scream an older woman came and held her until her crying and sobbing stopped. I was unable to imagine what could have happened that still clung, dragging such memories into their dreams.

In the mornings the women brought us milk and fresh bread and Abdulkader brought grapes and pomegranates from Bou Saâda. He sat with us, unable to stay away from Jamila. She was restless and her back ached. When I tried to rub it, she would get cross with me, telling me that I wasn't doing it like our mother. That I knew nothing about the discomfort of carrying a baby. She was missing our mother and the herbal teas and soothing massages she had been enjoying. At night she winced and turned, never quite settling in her sleep and I became increasingly afraid that the baby wouldn't wait for the danger to pass. Within a few days her pains increased and slowly settled into the early rhythms of labour, and we realised that it was time to find a woman to be midwife. Jamila was terrified, sad, tearful and very tired. At last, we decided that Abdulkader should return for our mother, and taking my camel he went back to fetch her. By the time our mother arrived the following morning my sister was flushed, rocking herself backwards and forwards and moaning softly. I had tried to entertain her, telling her the Tuareg stories I had learnt by our foster mother's campfire, but Jamila pushed me away and quietening herself went into the place where a woman hides inside her own body when the birth pains start to bring a baby.

My mother was quiet and patient. She talked away the pains when they came and was silent when the pains stopped. She gave my sister sips of pomegranate juice and camel's milk and pieces of sweet bread. I was bored of waiting and went to watch by the mouth of the cave.

The desert is very beautiful. It goes on forever, and I love its changing colours as the sun moves in the sky and is reflected in the sands. There are times when the desert and scrublands are almost white, and at other times they are orange and pink and seem to blossom with a fire from the world below. In the evening when the sky was the same indigo as Abdulkader's robes even the sand itself looked blue, as if it could gather all the Tuareg and protect them. Perhaps that is why they wear their indigo robes, because it hides them in the desert night, but perhaps they wear their indigo simply because it is beautiful. My mind wandered, but not so far that I didn't notice the distant stirring of the air above the desert. I ran to Abdulkader and pulled at his sleeve. He looked where I pointed and dropping the scabbard that he was polishing ran to the cave where my mother sat with Jamila. After whispering to my mother, he gathered Jamila, moaning into his arms. Wrapping her in a blanket he carried her from the mouth of the cave to a small hiding place hidden by shrubs in the high hollowed out bank of a dry riverbed. I followed and hid with them there. Then Abdulkader kissed my sister's forehead, held my mother briefly with his eyes and smiled at me before returning to where the camels grazed at the foot of the caves.

The desert night can hide a Tuareg but the brilliant blue of Abdulkader's shesh stood out against the sandstone hills. Perhaps that was his intention. Perhaps he planned to draw the soldiers away from us. He knew that they would not have forgotten the lone Tuareg murderer from Bou Saâda, so after hiding the three of us he took my beautiful white camel and set off quickly across the desert. Quickly, but not so fast that he wouldn't be seen, tracked and followed.

The soldiers arrived in a truck. A large, clumsy four-wheel drive that bounced across the hard ground spitting small rocks and stones. The truck screamed to a halt and twelve soldiers jumped out from beneath the canvas canopy one by one. I didn't watch anything after that.

Who knows if their actions were planned or authorised? Who knows what they intended? What I do know is that Abdulkader lit a fire under all of our tribe when he left. My sister, now in strong labour, stifled her moans with a piece of thick cotton and my mother prayed to our gods that the baby would wait just a little longer. It is a rare day when a mother hopes that her daughter's labour will last longer, and that the baby being born won't shout loudly in drawing its first breath.

We only heard what happened. We heard the soldiers telling the people of our tribe, our family, to go into the caves. We heard a struggle, and a bullet flying, and the sobbing cries of the women as they were pushed into the caves above us. We heard the sound of branches being dragged to build a fire and the crackling of flames as the dry wood caught. We smelt the fire, and then heard the ululating cry of desert women as they mourn, and even Jamila held her breath when we heard the women mourning themselves. After the cries fell silent, we heard the soldiers walking amongst the tents. The sound of jars smashing, and milk and water being poured into the sand. The sound of tearing as the tents were pulled down. The smell of bread and couscous being thrown onto the fire and the acrid smoke of burnt food.

We thought it was nearly over. We thought we were almost safe and that the soldiers might leave, when we heard the scrambling of boots against the riverbank. One of the soldiers had come to the dried riverbed, and I saw him standing there. I saw tears running down the dust on his face, and how he wiped them away with the back of his hand. I think he saw us, but he was young, and he had no appetite for death or what he had seen that day in the Naïll Mountains. He dropped the water canteen that he carried on his belt so that it landed inches away from my hand, and turning he left. I grabbed at the water, and after taking a sip we moistened Jamila's mouth.

We waited, barely breathing, wondering if the soldier would return but the engine on the truck grumbled back into motion and they were gone. As they left Jamila let out a loud moan, and there was a gush of water from between her legs. She put her hand there, and panicking drew her hand back.

'What is it, Mother?' she asked.

For the first time that day my mother smiled.

'It's your baby's head.'

Jamila turned to kneel, and after four or five pains

the baby's head was born, and my mother, pulling gently, delivered its small body.

I had not known that there is a moment when the world stands still before a baby cries. A moment when death and life are so close that they exist inseparable. I sat back on my heels. It had been for nothing. Jamila had carried this child, and gone through so much pain, but it had been for nothing. I looked at the small limp body, but my mother rubbed her knuckles down the baby's back, and flicked her fingers on the little feet, and then, as she rubbed at its small blue tinged body with a piece of canvas its little limbs contracted, it screwed up its face and shouted its indignation. My mother tied the cord with a piece of wool and cut it with a sharp clean knife before wrapping the baby and passing her to me.

Jamila lay back on the blankets sleeping for several minutes until the pain reached into her again, and the afterbirth followed the baby into this world. We gave Jamila the rest of the water, saving just a few sips for ourselves, and then our mother gathered her bundle. She told me not to go to the caves, and she set off on foot across the desert, following the tracks of the soldiers' truck.

I do not know if things would have been different if my mother had stayed with us, and I shall never know because I never found it in my heart to ask. What I do know is that when Jamila turned to me, to say that she felt wet, I had no knowledge of what could stop the red blood that pooled in the blankets. I wanted to push something up where the baby had been to stop the blood, but Jamila shook me away, so I lay beside her, the baby lying between us, and I held her hands, gazing to *memorise every line, each eyelash, the little flecks in the brown of her eyes.*

Each breath became more rapid and shallower as she closed her eyes, waiting for eternity. I don't know if she suffered but I think that she was peaceful as she fell asleep, in the hollowed-out bank of the river.

I was too scared to move, and I waited until it was dark, and then I went into the camp, and found the quiet burnt-out campfires, and the herd still bleating *and* baaing. *The camels were still alive. The French are idiots. They don't understand the value of a camel, but that was probably to the good of it, because if they had they would have shot them. I took the baby, filled a skin with milk from a goat with a new kid, and taking two of the camels I set off to find my mother.*

There are things that you never want to see, there are things better forgotten and not carried with us through our lives. I reached my mother at dawn, and found her sitting beside my beautiful, proud, broken, beloved brother-in-law. He was still alive. His arms and legs lay at odd angles, and his face was bruised and beaten. A pool of blood lay on his abdomen and was gathering the flies that follow death and dirt and poverty in the desert. He had been shot in the stomach. I took Jamila's baby and laid her gently beside her father. She was the last thing he saw.

My mother didn't ask about Jamila until Abdulkader had stopped breathing. I think she was scared to ask. I think she knew what had happened to Jamila before I told her. She had seen the blood covering my skirts and knew I would never have left Jamila if she were still alive.

In the desert you bury your dead quickly. Normally by sunset. We decided to go back to the caves, because we had to see, we had to make sure that there was no one left, and we had to bury my sister. Abdulkader wasn't tall, but he was lean and strong after years working metal and it was difficult to turn him to wrap his belly to stop the flies feeding in his blood. We used his scarf, and the soft oily dye turned my fingertips blue. I wished we had never returned and that we were back by the campfires with my foster mother, her silver rings bright against blue robes.

I tried to think about anything other than this task, in the place beyond the Naïll Mountains. I didn't want to think about my beautiful brother-in-law, and my sister lying dead in the dry riverbank. Instead, I thought of the silver being poured into moulds of sand, and the small triangles on the bracelets that I had decorated with hope. I thought about the long plaits my foster mother had made, when she had tried to make me look like a Tuareg girl. I thought about the long nights crossing the Great Sands as we travelled north across the Sahara. Then the baby started crying. We left her for a moment as we straightened Abdulkader's limbs. I ignored her for a few minutes more as I looked at his hands. His beautiful hands were bruised and distorted. I tried to pull his fingers straight, but the strong muscles only twisted and emphasised the broken bones, and knowing I was wasting time I left them. I have always regretted that I couldn't straighten the hands that made Jamila's bracelets.

We got the camel to lie on its belly and between us dragged Abdulkader onto the camel's back, tying him in place on top of the rugs with ropes from one of his saddlebags. We tied the camels together, and finally, gathering up his scattered belongings, we sat together for a few minutes.

I held Jamila's baby on my lap and my mother soaked a small piece of soft cotton in the goat's milk, trying again and again to squeeze it into the baby's mouth. The baby screamed louder and spat it out, and then I looked towards the camels. One of them was a mother whose calf had been left behind. My mother milked her and carrying it back in a bowl we shared some of the milk, and then I put my finger in the bowl and rubbed the baby's lips with the sweet warm liquid. She opened her eyes, looked at me, opened her mouth and turned towards my hand, searching for me. I gazed back at her and that was the first time that I understood that a woman can love a child she didn't bear, and that a child can grow inside your heart as well as beneath it.

'It looks as if you have just become the mother to this little one, Fatima.'

I looked up at my mother's face. I was confused. Why should I be her mother?

'I don't understand,' I said.

My mother was grey and tired and old in the fading light.

'I don't have the heart to raise another daughter in this world,' she said.

'We'll call her Aïcha after the Prophet's wife. The gods I prayed to weren't listening.'

Once the baby's little belly was full my mother helped me tie the baby across my abdomen and we travelled back to the camp in the Naïll Mountains. As we got nearer to the mountains the wind rose, and I thought that the sound of the winds against the caves would herald a sandstorm, but then I realised that the sound was not the wind. It was the sound of moaning coming from the cave. Dismounting, we dropped the camel ropes and after lowering Abdulkader's body onto the sand near the riverbed, we pulled his body straight before his muscles grew hard. Then we turned towards the mouth of the cave. The embers of the fires still gleamed, and my mother reached out and took my hand.

There are things that we carry into the rest of our lives which are best left behind, but I carry the sight of our friends, our family, our neighbours, the girls who had danced by the fire, the children, and those babies still in their mothers' arms. Some of their bodies were blackened with soot, and had been touched by the fires, but others had died contorted with terror as the fire and desert winds had sucked the air from the caves. We went carefully from one person to the next, despairing. We tapped them gently with the edge of our feet. Their bodies were fixed in the contortions of their death, and we thought that there was no hope for anyone, but then, after we had walked past, and through and over perhaps two hundred bodies – two hundred corpses from our tribe, recognising each one of them – I found where the moans were coming from. A woman lay in the furthest corner of the cave. She had hidden herself under thick brown rugs and was lying on the floor. It was her cries that I had heard. As I approached, my foot hit something made of metal, and her crying stopped, and the bundle of rugs seemed to grow smaller. I reached down, and pulled the rug back, to see the terrified face of a girl only a little older than me. It was Hayat.

I took Hayat's scarf and wrapped it across her face so that she couldn't see the faces of her father, mother, grandparents, brothers, sisters, aunts, cousins . . . She was the only member of her family to survive, and as I led her from the cave, she became my sister in much the same way that the baby became my daughter.

When the men from Bou Saâda came the next day, they counted two hundred and eighty-one bodies.

We did not spare Hayat from everything because she came to the riverbank and helped us to wash Jamila, her sister-dancer. We plaited Jamila's hair and washed the congealed blood from her lower back and legs. I remembered how she had hated the blue ink that stained her skin, and we went to the empty tent of one of the old women and found a pale blue dress and a dancer's veil.

I wanted to bury her with her bracelets, but my mother told us that one day we might need them to stay alive, and that Jamila had been a sensible girl and would have understood that we needed them more. I still wonder about that. I think my joyful, silly, vain sister would have wanted them. I took her veil and wrapped her bracelets, rings, necklaces, and the coins from her headdress in its soft folds before tucking them in the baby's blankets. The three of us carried Jamila's body to where we had left Abdulkader. We dug a shallow grave using our hands and a broken cooking pot, then lined it with Abdulkader's indigo cloak and lay Jamila and Abdulkader together as if it was their marriage bed. Covering them over with more cloth we hid them with the muddy sand of the Naïll Mountains, and while Hayat held the baby my mother and I fetched the biggest rocks we could carry and laid them over the grave so that no wild animals would disturb them in their sleep.

We made no plans that evening. We found a small tent that was still standing and found jars with dates, and flatbreads, and we wrapped ourselves in rugs and blankets and cuddled the baby. Our focus was entirely on the baby. We milked the camel and fed the baby little by little, dropping milk into her hungry mouth. She woke and gazed at me, her eyes beautiful and dark. That night when I slept, I put her against my skin to keep her warm, only waking when she wriggled, whimpering for more milk.

The morning after the massacre in the caves the men came from Bou Saâda. They had seen the French coming this way, and the smoke in the distance. They had waited, knowing that two such things together meant trouble.

We watched as the men started to fill the mouth of the cave with rocks before going to help. There were too many to bury in the dry hard land around us, so we left them where they had died and closed their grave with hands that were sore and bleeding from carrying the rocks and stones, but we didn't notice the pain. Our hands, like our hearts, were numb. After we had finished, we packed up all the tents and precious belongings of the men, women and children of our tribe. We helped to load the donkeys and camels and walked with the men from Bou Saâda back to the Medina. It wasn't a long journey when compared to months travelling south, but it was the most difficult, carrying the baby, but leaving my sister behind.

Hayat was calm, holding my mother's hand, but her eyes were glazed, and when I asked my mother why she wasn't crying my mother told me that sometimes when your heart is broken into too many pieces it takes a while before you can find tears again.

CHAPTER FOURTEEN

Grandmother is knocking on the door. I know it's her because she has a particular pattern. Two knocks. A gap. Two knocks. It isn't a request for entry. More a 'stand by your beds'. The door opens and Grandmother sticks her head in the door. Peering in to see what I'm up to. Checking that my room is neat and tidy. Making sure that I'm not back on the floor with Ali, I suppose. She's holding some sort of rose coloured bits and pieces. Nassima comes in behind.

'Can I come in?' Nassima says. I don't know why she bothers asking me.

I shrug. I have no choices left, so what does it matter? They've brought stuff. A long dress with an embroidered bodice. Some flat satin pumps. A hijab. All in a matching dusky pink. The dress was shop bought. Embroidered with a machine.

Ali's asleep on the floor in the hidden room and Nassima slides the cupboard back across the inner doorway. It slips into place without a sound. Nassima sits me on the stool next to my sewing table and starts dragging the hairbrush through my hair. Pulling it back, tight from my hairline, so that the scarf sits smooth. I hold Nassima's arm, balancing, as I step into the skirt that Grandmother is holding out in front of my feet.

'What's this for?' I pull at my skirts to straighten them so that they sit right.

'A surprise,' Nassima says as she kneels beside me. There's a lipstick in her hands. A rich plummy colour. She strokes at it with a small square tipped brush and then smooths the pigment, tickling onto my top lip. She smooths a thicker layer onto my lower lip. Then a little black kohl pencil is pulled smoothly across my lashes. Some eyeshadow is added. A necklace or two. Nassima lifts my hands, turning my wrists to fasten the little catches of two bracelets. Then they stand me, lift me from the chair, and I can see myself in a mirror. But I'm not sure it's me. Two years ago, when I first came, I looked like me. Curls all tangled. Jeans and beaded sandals. The navy-blue nail varnish was the first bit gone. Grandmother scrubbed my nails clean herself, the day I got here, a week after Mum died. And then the jeans were cut up into cleaning cloths, and she gave me a blue hijab to wear, because I was a woman now and should dress like one. But I still felt English. I was still me, but today I've disappeared, and an Algerian woman is staring back at me from the mirror.

'How can I get engaged with no fiancé?'

'We said he flew back to England to organize a job and somewhere to live for both of you,' Grandmother says.

'We told everyone you're in love. So sweet. In such a hurry to be married, so he went at once to find you somewhere. Wanting to please you,' Amti Nassima says.

'But why would he choose a place to live without me? Shouldn't I go too?'

Nassima shakes her head.

'It's a story. Just a story. To explain why he isn't here with you.'

Of course it's a story, but even in the story they've stolen my choices.

I go to the cupboard and pull the hidden door open. Ali winces as light floods back in, his pupils contracting against the light. He frowns when I walk in. He puts out a hand to touch the silk of my skirts.

'I'm sorry, Rabi.'

I look away from him, upwards to the arched ceiling, so that my tears don't spill out and ruin my makeup.

'Me too.' I say.

'You look . . . very Algerian,' he says.

'Don't I just?'

Nassima pulls me backwards and away. She checks me over like she checks her children before school on the first day of term.

'Lovely.' I walk beside her, round the balconies, down the stairs. The girl without a bridegroom. It says it all. Sums up all of the lies. A bride with no groom. A wedding night without sex. A marriage with no children. Plans for a divorce before the bride even gets snogged for the first time. What a mess. This is going to be a pathetic excuse of an engagement party. But

Nassima and my other Amtis have done their best. There are flowers, and the table is full of pastries and almonds. Bread rolls and cake fresh from Ali's bakery. Hibiscus cordial in glass jugs. There are even candles. That will be Nassima.

There are two seats next to the fountain. One for me. One for Ali. Miriam, his mother, sits in that one instead. Probably to annoy me. She smiles and takes my present from Amal. Tears the paper. I put my arm out to grab it back, but she slaps my hand away. She opens the paper, lifting a wooden box to show the other women. She opens it. Takes out sewing scissors. Pinking shears. Little pots of buttons and pins. A needle case, and a silver thimble. She passes each item to the other women. They touch everything. Turn each piece upside down to look more closely. I'm only given them back once everyone has stroked them, admired them, and covered them with fingerprints that have taken the shine off the scissors. I watch everything given but taken from me at the same time. Every single present is opened and touched by so many other people that nothing feels like mine. A bit like the fiancé I suppose.

Everyone reacts differently to this engagement.

Aïcha sits to one side of me, full of righteous satisfaction. She's done it. Got rid of me. Married me off. And for once she's pleased with me.

Nassima is shyly glad for me. As if this is something she had hoped for. She gave me a little parcel of lingerie earlier. Really? What do I need that for? Chocolate coloured silk with cream lace. Virginal white satin – well that's about right I suppose, and not a situation I'll be changing with Ali.

'Do you like them?' she asks. Doesn't she know that there's nothing in this engagement for me. Then I realise. She thinks that it might help Ali to, ew, to get interested.

'Thanks, Nassima.' I pick up the parcel, screwing the tissue paper round the lovely scraps inside so that no one will see; but Uncle Dahkman spots the parcel in my hands. He puts his hand on my shoulder, like he's consoling me. As if I've stuffed up an exam or the cat just got run over.

Miriam pretended to be friendly when she first saw me, but underneath you can tell she is pissed as hell. She gives me a hug and pushes an escaped curl back under the side of my hijab. She pats my cheek and smiles, but her smile doesn't reach her eyes, and the pat has a sting to it, where it's tender, where she slapped me yesterday.

I pretend it's a joy to me. This marriage. The wedding. As if I've found the perfect man. I'm pretending as hard as I can. Smiling till my cheeks hurt. They've come to look at Aïcha's idiot lamb. Except I'm not going to the butcher. He doesn't need any more wives. I am destined for the baker. The women are friendly, but I don't like the way they stare and whisper. They bring their little presents. A towel. Four tea glasses. A lamp. A little wooden photo frame. Well-meaning tat. I'll never be able to take all this stuff on the plane to England. I'll have to ship it or leave some other stuff behind.

The children *ooh* over my dress. A toddler, one of a neighbour's little girls walks towards me, stretching her sticky fingers towards the shine of silver thread. Nassima swoops with a fragment of a second to spare, swinging her above her shoulders so that the little one giggles and wraps her arms round her favourite amti; kissing her on the nose with one of the precious sticky kisses that you want to wipe off, but can't, in case you offend the little and beloved.

It goes on and on. I'm offered tea in Grandmother's best tea glasses. That's a first. Cousins bring me plates of food that I don't want to eat, and then eat the food on them themselves.

I've seen other girls at their engagement parties, and they are pink with blushes and smiles. They make sideways glances at the young men sitting beside them. They giggle and the men gaze at them. Because the girls are perfect. Joyful. Theirs.

Today it's my turn. I don't want to eat anything and even I think I am suspiciously quiet. Grandmother starts to frown each time she looks at me. I think she's expecting me to start to scream, or cry, or insult Miriam. I'd rather tap dance on the stairs. No one mentions Ali. No one has even said his name. Inspiration! So I will. I stand. Miriam looks up at me from my latest present – another wooden zviti bowl – and hisses, yes hisses, 'What do you think you're doing?'

'Giving a speech.' My sister puts a hand on the top of my arm.

'Are you supposed to?'

'No, I'm not.'

'Oh.' Amal lets go of my arm.

'Dear friends, I want to thank you on this special

day for coming to look at me in my beautiful dress. Thank you for my presents. Thank you for helping with this feast and for bringing all your children, parents and third cousins.' Mani looks agitated and Nassima has her hands over her eyes, as if she wants to listen but can't quite bear to watch.

'Today would have been even more special if Ali had been here, but he has gone to find us somewhere in England because we'll be happier . . . happy where we grew up.' Mani has put her hands on her hips and is glaring at me. But she can't actually stop me.

'It is so sad that people are missing today.' Nassima kicks the back of my foot, beneath the dress, so that no one can see.

'I know Mum and Dad would have had a lot to say about me getting engaged. And Ali is devastated that his best man won't be with him.'

Mani can't bear any more and starts clapping. She grabs a cup cake and almost rams it between my lips, calling, 'Dahkman. Your speech now,' and as I swallow the cake, crumbs dry in my mouth, I whisper, 'because your bastard husbands killed him.'

Dahkman says the right things. He smooths the ruffles and praises Miriam for her cakes and bread rolls and lastly for her son, good, honourable Ali. The room quietens at this. So he stops there.

That's the speeches then. Definitely time to stop.

The musical choices are loud and traditional and what ear plugs were invented for. My dad loved this stuff, but he only played it when Mum was out at work because it gave her a headache. Mani is dancing with her hands, like a Tuareg, and Dahkman and some of my uncles stand together before forming a line and starting to dance. It's a bit like Greek dancing, I suppose, but they are smiling and engaged. Strutting, laughing, mimicking each other. I sit and watch. Amal comes and sits on the arm of my throne-for-a-day chair, and I lean my head against her ribs and it's surprising how peaceful I feel. As if every bit that could fight has been drained from me.

'Did you have an engagement party in England?'

'I had lots of things in England.'

The evening wanes and sleepy children are carried up to bed. Women put the leftover food in plastic pots, emptying the dishes of the feast. One by one my cousins extinguish the candles, and then someone, I'm too tired to care who, leads me back to mine and Amal's room. I realise it is Nassima, and she sits with me while I undress, and then tucks me under the red blankets like a poorly child. I wait till she's gone and walk on bare dirty feet to the next room, where I lie down next to Ali and pull the blanket over us both.

CHAPTER FIFTEEN

There are advantages to sleeping with Ali. The warmth mainly, and two blankets would seem to be better than one; and as I've said before, he smells nice. The disadvantage to sleeping with Ali is that until we get married sleeping with him doesn't include a bed. I'm not ignoring the obvious, but the words *sex* and *Ali* don't belong in the same sentence.

The floor becomes progressively harder because a sleeping twenty-four-year-old has stolen all the covers and is starting to lean on me. Time to get up and go back to my bed; but Amal is lying flat on her back. A snoring starfish. So, back into Cinderella mode. I hesitate for a moment before pinching Amal's jeans and one of her T-shirts. I screw my hair up on top of my head with a scrunchie. I go to the mirror. I'd forgotten the makeup. The Algerian girl looks back at me from the mirror. She's a mess. Not the polished almost-bride from yesterday.

Flapping the black bin bag open I start on the

courtyard, in a corner under the arches, picking up sweet wrappers and some plastic cola bottles that the older children discarded. I'm glad I started early. There are glasses and teacups, and plastic beakers to gather. How can so many women be so untidy when it would be so easy, so quick, to sort this out themselves? The washing up bowl is empty in the sink. Putting it against one hip I grab a plastic laundry basket. There are teddies by the stairs and some red plastic cars have been lined up on the table. I gather the toys into the basket. The palace is waking up as I finish. I can hear the children up on the balcony, the doorbell rings upstairs. Grandmother calls 'Saha' to an uncle.

I boil some water in the saucepan and find the cups for tea. Grandmother blocks the light in the doorway for a moment before coming to sit at the table. 'You've been busy,' she says in almost praise. 'Go rest.'

I take the tea and go to sit cross-legged on the floor next to an archway. I shut my eyes, looking forward to a day wandering down to the harbour after these quiet minutes. Then a metallic tapping starts. There's probably a problem with the plumbing again. Someone's bashing the pipe below a blocked sink perhaps. But it goes on and on. *Tap-tap.* An irritatingly persistent metallic woodpecker somewhere in the palace. It carries on, but the sound seems to get louder and louder. Sighing I open my eyes and look around. The noise is coming from the fountain.

The fountain. Someone's mending it, or destroying it, or working on the plumbing beneath the tarnished copper tiers. Dad? Is Dad back? It's the sort of thing Dad does. Turn up as if he's never been away. Start fixing things, mending things. He is always in a hurry, and about to leave again. I stand, so quickly I nearly lose my balance. I run to the other side of the fountain to the cupboard thing where you can climb underneath. There are legs sticking out. Jeans. Black boots like Dad wears.

'Dad?' I grab his ankle. 'Is that you?' There's a thump inside the cabinet, and a very English, very London voice mutters, 'Oh, fucking shit.' Then the legs, torso, arms and legs wiggle out towards me like some sort of odd breech birth. It's not Dad.

'Oh.' I sit back heavy on the fountain's wall. So disappointed. I had thought, hoped, for just those moments, that Dad was back. He'd solve everything. Rescue me and take me home.

A young man rolls onto his knees and standing, moves in front of me.

'Are you okay?' he says. He's nursing one hand in the other and has a red mark on his forehead.

'Oh, shit.' I rush to the kitchen and soak a tea towel in cold water.

'What's that for?' Grandmother asks.

'I've just hurt the plumber.'

Grandmother sighs and pours herself more tea. The man is sitting by the cupboard now. I give him the cloth.

'For your head. Sorry.'

And he smiles. It's a bit of a wonky smile, and there's a shine in it.

'I've done worse. Had no idea that fixing the fountain would be so dangerous. Aïcha didn't warn me how pretty the girls are here.'

I tut. Any minute now he'll be asking if I have sisters as beautiful as me. It's a standard question round here, when men start flirting.

'I thought you were Mokhi Kateb. The last time the fountain got fixed it was him.' I don't know why I don't just say my dad fixed it, but I don't. He'll have worked that out, won't he?

'He did a good job. I can see where he soldered the new pipes, but something has eaten through the pump mechanism, and it must have leaked. I reckon it's doable though.' He smiles again. His smile is still a bit wonky as he brushes his hair back from his face, leaving some greasy slime on his forehead.

'You've got little hands. You can probably give me a hand if Aïcha hasn't got you too busy today.'

There is probably a reason why lying in the cupboard under a fountain is more tempting than sitting at a table outside a café, by the harbour, in the sun. I suspect it's because I'm eighteen and he has no more than five years on me.

I have to lie on my back under the central pipes and reach up. It is filthy. I take a small chisel and start to chip away, keeping my lips firmly shut so that flakes of dirt don't fall into my mouth. By the time I've cleaned it I'm covered in muck and grease. He helps me out of the cupboard and starts laughing.

'You are quite gorgeous. A pearl amongst women.'

I shove the chisel back in his hand, and strop back to the kitchen. Even Grandmother looks surprised at the state I'm in.

'What have you been doing?'

'I helped clean the cupboard beneath the fountain.'

'Oh,' she says.

Back to the mirror upstairs. I'm covered in grime. The kohl is smudged, and I look like a bedraggled panda. Amal wakes up to see me standing there and she blinks. As if she's not sure whether she's woken up or not. Then she laughs, great giggling laughs that tumble through her. Ali appears at the doorway. It's the first time I've seen him standing since we dragged him there, to lie on the floor. He looks horrified.

'Grief, Rabi. What have you done to my fiancée?'

So we sit laughing. As if the world is ending and laughing is the only thing we can do. Ali can't stand for long. He pushes himself towards the bed, holding the wall for support. He smiles at Amal.

'You see why I like men then?' He grimaces when she punches him.

I don't want to go to the harbour. I'd planned today with Amal. She was going to sit with Ali and make sure he was okay so that I could get some fresh air. But now I just want to go back and see what's happening with the fountain. As if it's the fountain I'm interested in.

I have a shower. Wash my hair until it squeaks and brush it smooth. Scrub my face with a flannel until I've got the makeup off. And the grime. I put on a cotton skirt. A white blouse. A hijab. Who's in my mirror this time? A young woman. Devout. Wholesome.

Grandmother looks up when I walk into the kitchen.

'That's better. Go give Khalid a cup of coffee.'

'Who?'

'The man repairing the fountain.'

So, I have his name. I get my sweet pea mug, and fill

it with coffee, hiding the pattern from Grandmother.

He's stopped working and is sitting on the floor by the wooden door to the space beneath the fountain. I give him the cup, speaking Tamezight. He replies in the same language. He doesn't really look at me. He should apologize for teasing me.

'Thanks. I thought that servant girl would have brought me the coffee.' Servant girl. I shouldn't be surprised. I was clearing up, hair everywhere, and filthy. Maybe it's a good thing that he doesn't know who I am.

'She's not here.' He looks up and smiles.

'Shame. She was helping me. Is she back tomorrow?' Idiot. He still hasn't recognized me.

'She's here every day.'

'Is she English?'

'Half English.' He blows on the coffee for a moment, and then takes a mouthful.

'Thanks for the coffee.' He picks up a wrench and crawls back in the cupboard.

CHAPTER SIXTEEN

Next morning I'm up at six. I take a kohl pencil from Amal's bag and draw lines above and below my eyes. I don't bother brushing my hair, just scrunch it up again, like the day before, and taking Amal's jeans from the wash pile I head back to the courtyard. He's back at seven.

'I thought you might like some help. Like you said I've little hands.' He smiles that wonky smile.

'I asked for you yesterday, but you'd gone home. You can help if you want. But we can tidy the courtyard first. I wouldn't want to get on the wrong side of Aïcha Kateb by not letting you finish your work.'

I fetch the washing up bowl, and we gather the cups and mugs. He puts the kids' toys in the toy box and helps me sweep the courtyard. We don't say much, but when I catch his glance there's that smile. Each time. It doesn't take long, and after I've grabbed a cup of tea I go and sit beside the little doorway, finding tools from his tool kit and passing them to him. I like the feel of the skin of his hand when I pass him the hammer and the new bits of pipe. He asks me to pass a pot of grease, and the wrench again, and there's a squeaking noise, and the sound of water. I stand to see if the fountain is working at last, but the water isn't coming from there. He wriggles out from the cupboard, and he is dripping with water the colour of rust.

'Truly a treasure among men.' And I giggle, the sort of giggle that comes out when you haven't had anything to really laugh about for a long time, when the sun seems brighter, and the winter is over, and you've just spotted the first daffodils. There's that wonky grin again, and he grabs my wrists and shakes his hair. Did I mention the hair? Lots of it. Dark and curly and kind of shiny, except it is filthy dirty and a bit slimy right now. He shakes his hair like a dog so that the droplets are sprayed all over me. And he turns my wrists, so that my hands are in his, and he bends forward to whisper, 'You're lovely.'

I'm sure that blushing doesn't suit me, but there's not much I can do about it. It's then I hear Grandmother talking to Amti Nassima upstairs.

'Got to go. See you tomorrow?' And I'm gone.

After my shower I scrub off the makeup and put on the same skirt and blouse as the day before and spend the day in my room sewing the beads on my wedding dress and thinking about Khalid. If Ali was any other sort of bridegroom, I'd probably feel guilty, but I don't, and embroider a little frog near the hem. Because it kind of fits. What with the slime an all.

Day three. Dad didn't take this long to fix the fountain. I go downstairs at six again and start tidying up. He arrives at seven, just like yesterday.

'How are you doing?'

'I should get it finished today.'

'Are you going to sort out the boiler as well?'

'Would you like me to?'

'It'd be nice. To have hot water all day.'

He takes my hand and moves to kiss the back of it, but I snatch it back.

'Stop it. I'll get in trouble.'

'Have you worked here long?'

'I've been here for two years. But I'm a seamstress really.'

'You're young to be a seamstress, aren't you?'

'Not really. I've been sewing since I was little. My mum taught me. I used to be a waitress at one of the hotels, but then I got a job in the sewing room.'

'So why are you here then?' I don't have an answer, so decide it's better not to reply.

'Tea or coffee?' He sits down on the wall round the fountain.

'Tea.'

'Haven't you got any family?'

'What do you mean?'

'Well, if you were mine . . . my daughter or sister . . . I wouldn't make you work for Aïcha. I'd want more for you.'

'I'd love to be looked after like that.'

He's not smiling now, and he's looking at my mouth like he's never seen a mouth before and doesn't know quite what to do with one.

'Tea.'

He's back in the cupboard when I get back with the

drinks.

'Do you want to clean the tiles in the pool?'

'Clean them?'

'I gave a bit of them a scrub yesterday. They used to be coloured. Blue with flowers. I think it will be quite special. Really nice for Aïcha's granddaughter when she gets married. You could get candles for it as well. But first the tiles need cleaning.'

Grandmother doesn't look surprised when she sees me kneeling with a scrubbing brush in the fountain. I'm sure that I look more surprised when she goes into the kitchen and brings me a new packet of yellow dishwashing gloves and a tube of cheap hand cream. She smothers the cream into the palm of my hands, and I rub it in before pulling the gloves on.

'A bride shouldn't have ugly hands.'

'Thank you.'

It feels comfortable. Warm somehow. Working on the tiles while Khalid taps away under the fountain, trying to fix the pump. Companionable.

I've never seen the patterns in the pool before. They must have been there since the fountain was made. There are white tiles with indigo and turquoise flowers, swallows with red markings on their necks, and stars and geometric lines hidden behind a crust of sand and dirt. It is painstaking work, rubbing the silty dirt back into a paste so that I can mop it up. I rinse the cloth in clean water and after the cloth is dirty ring it out in a second bucket. Every hour or so Khalid stops and comes and sits on the wall for a few minutes, stretches his shoulders and goes to empty the dirty bucket before bringing me the same bucket back, full of clean fresh water. He doesn't say much. The courtyard is getting hotter, we're getting tired.

'Do you want a coffee when we finish here?'

Oh yes. I do. But I won't.

'I can't. I'm sorry. I will have other things to do later.'

Khalid mutters something.

'What?'

'They make you work too hard.'

'I don't mind.'

'You should.'

We carry on working. It's early afternoon when I finish, and Grandmother comes to look at the fountain.

'I had no idea,' she says. She strokes the tiles round the edge with a sort of reverence. 'It was already covered when I came to live here.' Then, almost like waking up, she looks at me. 'Go have a shower. You're filthy.'

When I take the gloves off my hands, my skin feels soft, and the dry tough skin has been rubbed into a white paste. The shower is cold, but it feels good to wash the dirt off, and brush the dust from wet hair before rinsing it again. I plait it before it has a chance to frizz.

Ali is asleep on my bed. He has started walking more, but he still hasn't left my room. It's one of only a few rooms that has its own bathroom, so that isn't a problem, but he has started to look restless. We will have to get married quickly. He can't stay here for much longer because the little ones won't keep a secret if they realise Ali is living here. And the little ones notice everything.

Bird is still in his cage. He bashes himself against the side of the cage when he sees a cloud of goldfinches above him, but settles when I give him some seed, and refill his water from the glass beside the bed. I grab a book. Jane Eyre. And sit with my back to the wall, and my legs over Ali's legs. After a while he fidgets and pushes my legs back, waking himself up.

'You're back. I was getting bored,' he says.

'So I'm in Algeria to keep you company, am I?' He sits up, wincing.

'I hurt.' What do I say to that? His bruises have turned yellow, and his stitches have been taken out. I don't know if his pain is physical, or emotional. I don't think he would be complaining if it was just his body hurting.

'Grandmother has got someone to repair the fountain.'

'Nice.' He rolls back onto his back and shuts his eyes. I want to tell him about Khalid, but I don't know how to. Because it means I'm happy when he isn't. It seems wrong to tell the man I'm marrying that I think I'm falling in love.

CHAPTER SEVENTEEN

Grandmother's wedding plans make me want to wriggle free. I don't know how else to explain it. I don't think that it is because I'm marrying Ali, in fact that probably helps because he understands the wanting to wriggle free feeling as well. I think the questions bug me most. 'What is your dress like?' 'Are you having flowers?' 'What is the cake like?' 'When is it?' I feel like printing a leaflet with answers, and gaps for suggestions so that I don't have to get the same advice over and over.

Miriam keeps visiting Grandmother, telling her plans. She has started to complain that she needs Ali to decorate the cake, but some of his fingers were broken so he won't be kneading bread or doing sugar icing for a while. She will have to pay someone. She keeps on asking to see my dress, but I can't bear her chubby fingers touching it, so I say it is a surprise. She smells like the bakery, like Ali, but there is something sour about Miriam. Probably her face. When will she understand that the heart loves what it loves? That I couldn't have got Ali to fall in love with me, even if I wanted him to.

Nassima and Amal are embroidering tablecloths. Amal keeps on pricking her fingers. She's sucking her finger again.

'Come and help me,' she says.

I want to be out by the fountain, but I sit at the table with Amal. She's really making a pig's ear out of it. If she was one of the kids at the Embroidery School, I'd be snipping out her stitches and making her start again. I try to show her how to hold the thread against the needle so the silks don't twist, but she still can't get it right. I let her carry on.

Grandmother, who was smiley and happy when I agreed to marry Ali, is beginning to look less smiley. I'd like to think she has started to realise what a mistake this is. That I'm being used to save face and keep everyone else happy. When I catch her doing it for the fifth time in half an hour I ask why.

'What do you keep looking at me for?'

She frowns and looks down at the bread she's kneading.

'You remind me of someone. I keep on seeing her in your face.'

'Who?'

'My Mum's cousin, Amti Hayat.' An answer like that normally brings a story, but Grandmother knocks the dough onto the baking tray and slams the oven door. We're not getting a story today.

***

I'm back at the fountain at seven. Khalid arrives at the same time. He smiles when he sees me. I've already tidied up the courtyard and made us tea.

'I think I've fixed it,' he says.

I wish he hadn't, because I won't see him again once he's finished.

He goes to the cupboard, and fiddles around for a bit. And it starts. A trickle from a pipe at the side. Some dirty water comes out before it starts to run clear. He turns the water off and gets some old towels to soak up the dirty water. Then he turns the water back on. I take off my sandals and roll my jeans to my knees, putting my feet in the water. It inches up my legs until it reaches just below the top of the pool. I want to sit here forever. I pretend I'm Khalid's bride, and that the fountain has been cleaned for our wedding. I want to watch our children playing in the pool when we visit each summer. I'm startled when I'm splashed with some drops of water.

'Penny for them?'

'My thoughts are worth more than pennies.' And I smile at him, and he does his funny lop-sided grin thing back at me, so I stand in the pool, and he holds out his arms to help me out. It's an easy thing to stand in his arms, and to raise my face for his kiss.

'Rabia!' He's so startled by Grandmother's voice that he slips and actually drops me in the pool. If it was just Khalid I'd laugh, but Grandmother has thunder in her voice.

'Go and get dry.' I stand and climb out the pool. Khalid doesn't touch me or help me this time.

'Yes, Grandmother.'

Khalid looks down at me. 'Grandmother?'

I shrug and walk away, trailing water in the dust behind me.

When I get back to my room, I shove Ali off the bed.

'Go and sit in your cupboard. I'm getting dressed.' I plait my hair, and dress in the skirt and blouse. Put on my scarf. I slide the cupboard back open.

Ali is waiting. Looking worried.

'Grandmother caught me kissing the plumber.' I know Ali isn't the husband of my dreams, but he doesn't have to laugh.

'The plumber? Nasty smelly things, plumbers. Why do you want to kiss one of them when you can have me?' But he stops teasing me when he realises that I'm crying. And then he hugs me.

'I think it's time Ali gets home from England.'

He walks downstairs with me. He comes with me to the fountain. Khalid is clearing up his tools, and the fountain is running. I am disappointed to see it working, that I missed it starting up again. Ali goes over to Khalid and holds out his hand, 'You've done a good job. It'll be lovely for the wedding. I'm Ali. This is Rabia, my fiancée.'

Khalid looks at me. This time he sees me, in spite of the scarf. His eyes narrow.

'Oh, yes. Rabia. She helped me clean the fountain.'

Ali looks at Khalid. At the naked fury in his eyes.

'Fancy a coffee, Rabi?' Ali asks. He wanders off, leaving us alone.

'You're the bride? Why didn't you say?' Khalid asks.

There's only one honest answer: 'I didn't want to.'

'You should have said.'

Khalid's gone by the time Ali comes back.

***

Khalid is waiting for me in the courtyard the next morning.

'Rabia.'

'Hi.' I stand in front of him. Head bowed, hands joined, twisting behind my back. Miserable.

'I wouldn't have encouraged you, asked you to help me if I'd known you were engaged. I've come to say goodbye, and to say sorry. But I need to talk to you too. Sit down.'

I sit. Obedient, disempowered and fed up.

'I wouldn't have tried to kiss you.'

'You didn't kiss me.'

'But I was planning to!'

I look up at him, try to look encouraging. It seems to work.

'Rabia! Stop. You aren't helping.'

I make a noise. A kind of 'tant-pis' noise. A gallic 'too bad'.

'If you're marrying Ali because you want to that's fine. I'll go. You'll never see me again, but I've heard things. And look, I grew up in England.'

'Like me.'

'Like you, and I'm not condemning the man. I've no problem with him. But did you know he's gay?'

'He's not gay. He's downright miserable at the moment.'

'Rabia.' He looks cross now. As if he wants to say

1 4 6

much more. Then he pauses, as if I'm the village idiot and really don't know what I'm talking about.

'He's gay. Homosexual. He likes men.'

'He likes me.'

'Rabia.' He hits his fist onto the wall round the fountain, cracking a tile, and then grabs his hand in the other and looks at his knuckles. 'Ow.'

'He shouldn't be marrying you. He shouldn't be marrying anyone. You won't want to hear this, but I heard he had a lover, they were caught together . . .'

I've had enough.

'Do you think I'm so ignorant? So stupid? I know about them. I saw Saïed die. I saw them beating up Ali. You didn't see. You weren't there. I thought they were going to kill him, but when Grandmother told them that I was marring him they stopped and went away. If I don't marry him, they'll come back, and they won't be stopped next time.'

'But you can't spend your life married to Ali.'

'He'll take me back to England.'

'I could do that.'

'What? You'd marry me instead? To save me from Ali?'

He pauses. Looks at me for a fraction too long. 'I could.'

'We've known each other five minutes.'

'Trust me it feels longer right now.'

'It would feel much longer if we didn't get on.'

'We'd get on. You know we would.' It's tempting. So tempting. But I won't.

'Will you kiss me?'

Khalid looks at me and sighs. 'No.'

Well, I didn't expect that.

'Why not?'

'You aren't mine to kiss.' And that's what gets me. Really pisses me off.

'I'm not anyone's to kiss. I don't belong to anyone. I don't belong to you, or to Ali, or to Grandmother. None of you can choose for me.'

'But now you know about Ali, surely . . .'

'I've always known about Ali. I always knew.'

'So why?'

'Because I love him.' That shuts him up. He stops trying to argue with me.

'So that's a no then. And if I kissed you? Would it change your mind?'

Oh yes. It might. I might change my mind for a kiss. I might change my mind for a kiss that he'd take without asking for permission. I might change my mind if he held me in his arms for long enough. I might. If the kiss was grabbed. Stolen.

'I don't want you to kiss me.'

'You did two minutes ago.'

'A woman's prerogative.'

Khalid looks at me and pulls a face. Then he looks at his bruised knuckles. 'I wish I hadn't done that. I think I've broken something.'

'You probably have.'

That's when I realise Ali is standing on the top floor of the balconies, watching us. He starts to walk down, slowly circling us. Khalid is frozen like some sort of prey, until Ali comes to stand in front of us.

'You're playing with fire, little Rabia,' Ali says.

'You have a choice,' Khalid says.

The girls at home would be so impressed. I have two men. Two good, nice looking Algerian men who want to marry me. And either could take me home to England. Either could get me out of here, and away from Grandmother. Then I suddenly, in my head, see Saïed lying on the ground, smashed. If I marry Ali, I can keep him safe. Protect him from that. Look after him while he mends.

'I have a choice. And I've already made it.' I rest my hand on Ali's chest. Khalid doesn't have a jacket or tool kit with him today. He just stands up and walks away.

The door slams upstairs, and Ali pulls me into a hug, inside the circle of his arms.

'What happened?'

'He said he'd marry me, so I wouldn't have to marry you.' Ali doesn't say anything. And I start crying. Big noisy sobs. The sort of big noisy can't breathe sobs you make when you are broken. When something really hurts. When you're shattered in the middle with no hope of repair. And I don't know how to stop.

'Why didn't my dad come back? It would have been okay if he'd come back.'

'I need you, Rabi. We'll be okay together.'

'I don't want to spend my life being okay.'

'You have a choice, Rabi.'

'No, I don't.' The tears come back, and the sobbing isn't stopping this time.

Grandmother comes and pats me on the back and says nice things to try and calm me. Then she says not such nice things. She tries slapping my face, which doesn't surprise me. I'm a bit surprised when she pours a glass of cold water over my head, but I just feel even more miserable, and my sobs get louder and even more out of control.

So Grandmother fetches Amti Nassima. Nassima gets a towel and starts drying my hair. She croons to me as if I were her little daughter, but the miseries come back harder. And my sobbing gets louder.

'I miss my mum.'

So Grandmother fetches Amal who comes downstairs in pyjamas, pulling on a dressing gown. She sits and looks at me. Grandmother and Nassima sit and look at me too. Amal carries on looking at me, but the longer I cry the more bored she looks and starts tapping her feet. 'Oh, do shut up, Rabia,' she finally says. 'You don't have a monopoly on misery. Look at me. I've run away from home.'

Well that worked. I sniff a bit more but stop crying.

'Really?' I ask.

Grandmother and Nassima shove me towards the stairs. Grandmother pushes me. Nassima pushes Amal.

'Go upstairs and tell her all about it, Amal.'

So, Amal and I go upstairs. Amal knows all the important stuff about me, whether I want her to or not. Now it's my turn to find out about her.

She sits me down on the bed. The mattresses are back in the room and the inner room is hidden behind the cupboard once more. The pile of thin mattresses has been divided in two, and the table has Amal's perfume and hand cream sitting next to my cahiers. It looks like there have always been two of us in here. She reaches into her bag and pulls out a packet of jelly babies. She passes me one and then starts to dig around in the packet. Reaching to the bottom of it she pulls out two rings and puts them on the fourth finger of her left hand. They aren't 'marrying your childhood sweetheart who saved up for two months' kind of rings. They are the sort of rings given to a girl by a man with money. Shining white with diamonds. She holds her left hand out in front of her, changing the angle to look at the light refracting through it.

'We met at my college art exhibition.'

'Who's we?'

'Me and Iain. My husband. It was flattering. He buys art for people. He's well known in that world. He's got a good eye. And I was flattered because he wanted to buy my series of paintings. He collected them, and somehow, he managed to collect me too. It was lovely. At first. Iain Connaught's wife. Everyone was interested in me. Everyone wanted to talk to me, and be nice, but then I started to see that they just wanted to be noticed by him. He had trouble selling my work, trouble convincing people that my work was worth investing in, so in his head he moved on. He found other artists. New bright hopes of the Royal Academy, more mature painters whose work was already valued. And I got in the way. Annoyed him. I'd stopped working by then too. And while I needed him more, he needed me less, I suppose. He travelled more, without me. And then when he did come home, he didn't want to talk to me. Or be with me. And then he didn't come home when he wasn't travelling. He started selling new artists and stopped inviting me to the shows and exhibitions. So I knew it was time to leave. He didn't need me anymore. And there was no one who would care if I did or didn't stay. And I came here because I thought I might find someone who would care, and I found you. And Grandmother. And the others.'

I'm too tired to cry anymore. I needn't have worried. I'm stuck with her. Amal won't be going anywhere.

'What will you do when I go back to England?'

She shrugs slightly, 'I haven't decided.'

CHAPTER EIGHTEEN

The preparations continue. There's a gathering period before an Algerian wedding, where the women collect the things the bride will need, and traditionally prepare for her move to her mother-in-law's home. Miriam comes every day, and bosses me about. You'd think that she would have been more tolerant of me. I thought she liked me, but she still needs someone to blame, and the convenient someone just happens to be me. She had always thought that I would be Ali's wife one day, even when we were kids in England. She had enjoyed teaching me to cook, believing that she was teaching me to be a good wife to her son. She had watched our friendship, expecting it to be the foundation of a marriage when we were old enough. Now she looks at me and I can hear her in my head saying, 'What a waste of all my time. You're not enough for a man like my son. You were never going to be enough.'

The thing that troubles me most is the dress. I've

spent months on the wedding dress, and I've always planned on using it as an example of my work. It uses English images on a garment with an Algerian structure. It's my passport to university. The proof that I should get a place studying textiles and design. If I wear it, I can still do that, but it feels too special for a wedding like this. Like mine. So I'm borrowing Nassima's wedding dress. Grandmother doesn't get it. She's watched me sew every day, and now I don't want to wear a dress that is almost complete and almost perfect. I tell her it's a tradition to borrow something old, and that Nassima's dress is my something borrowed. Amal is going to lend me a necklace with a small sapphire in its pendant. My blue. And my new can be the underwear Nassima bought me. Sorted. I don't need to do much. The other women love weddings and have started cooking and baking. Dahkman bought a new chest freezer, and it's buzzing away in the kitchen while it is slowly filled with wedding food. The neighbours have started bringing tubs with flowering plants. They have little paper stickers so that we know who to give them back to. The jasmine that grows up the bannisters is starting to blossom. It's lovely. It will be perfect. Smell heavenly. But it annoys me, as if there's a conspiracy against me. Even the flowers are drawing me into the wedding. I can't pretend it is real though. I don't want to pretend it's real. It's a masquerade, and just part of my escape route home.

Ali left today. He went to the bakery. I went with him because he's safer if he looks like a man with his fiancée. Once he's there I continue down to the sewing shop. It might be years before I can come back. There will be sewing shops in England, but there is something about the fabrics and embroidery silks here that is uniquely Algerian, and I'm going to miss it. I can't afford to buy anything, but the ribbons and coloured cottons sooth me.

I've stopped sewing my dress because there's no point, and it's packed in one of my two suitcases. Amal is going to bring a case with my wedding presents when she comes back to England, but for now she's staying put.

Nassima's dress is hanging from the curtain rail, and there are packets of new makeup from Amal. Growing up I imagined sitting with my mum on the night before my wedding. I sit with Amal instead. Nassima offered to talk to me about 'marriage', but I said no, and Amal told her we had already had a chat. For tonight the thing I want most is to finish Fatima's story before I go back to England. I wanted to take Amal to the mountains, to Bou Saâda. There's no time for that, but I can give her the story.

Amal is sitting on the windowsill next to Bird. She is dribbling bird seed from her fingers into the seed pot. Bird is hopping onto his perch and to the bottom of the cage and back again, pecking at the small black seeds. I get the fourth cahier.

'Was there much more? After they rescued their cousins?' It's the best bit of the day, sharing the story of our women. It soothes me, like the time spent with Fatima soothed me as a child.

'The story changes a bit here. I was a bit older. Fatima became more open about things. About what happened.' I've caught Amal's attention, and smile to myself as I find the ribbon marking our place in the small exercise book.

We were the only survivors from the mountain and were welcomed because hospitality is a rule in these lands; but while they smiled at our faces the women whispered behind our backs and avoided us when they could. We knew that we were lucky to have survived, but they thought we were unlucky because we were people who had lost so much. When we told the women that we wanted to go north to the city their faces shone with sorrow and relief. Without us they could forget what had happened and the bad luck would leave with us.

Three silversmiths had planned on travelling to Algiers to trade with the French, and we made a deal with them. We would sell them our camels when we reached the city in return for some of their silver. The camels would be no use to us in the city, but we made a poor bargain, and the men knew that. We took a small sturdy goat that was good for milk and tied our bundles together. As the camels swayed to their feet, I held tight to the baby strapped to my chest, and from the height of the camel I looked down on the people of the Ouled Naïll who came to say goodbye. Their faces pretended a sorrow that didn't extend to their eyes. I wondered if they would sweep our footprints away.

It was a long journey, but when Algiers finally came into view, we saw her rising from the hills beside the sea. Her creamy buildings blended the old Ottoman city with the French buildings nearer the harbour. She was beautiful, and I imagined her as a lovely woman, full of promises. She kept some, she broke some, but she was a woman. She made her choices, and sometimes our White Lady brings a blessing, and sometimes she brings a curse.

When we arrived in the city we parted ways with the silversmiths, hid our silver in our clothing, and stood in the marketplace, three country women standing uncertain in the middle of a souk with strange words all around us. I had never seen so many people, and I had never seen people treating each other with such indifference. They pushed past us, almost knocking me over, even with a baby in my arms. Hayat held close to my mother, turning towards her when she saw French soldiers in the square, and closing her eyes. People were speaking French, but we had never needed to learn. A man wandered over to us. He spoke a Berber language. Now that we understood. We explained that we had come to Algiers. Were there Ouled Naïll here? He looked at us differently. Less kindly.

'Ouled Naïll?' He took a scrap of paper from his pocket and with a small, chewed pencil drew directions for us. 'You'll find them here.' He pointed and drew a large arrow. We had no idea that we had asked where to find the whores of the city. We still looked lost, and the man showed us a little mercy.

'My son has a lot of work to do today, but for some silver he can take you.'

We gave away the first of the precious silver that was to fall like sand through our fingers and followed the child from the wide streets with strange square writing through the maze of the Casbah. We had heard of the Casbah, and been told it was some sort of paradise, but what we found were high-walled alleys stinking of rubbish, and steps turning left and right, leaving us with no sense of direction. When we arrived at the Rue des Ouled Naïll we gave the boy his silver and looked around us.

We saw young women standing around in doorways, hiding the smell of the streets with cigarettes and the smell of strong coffee. Some were dressed in the heavy layered dresses, silver coins and veils of the Ouled Naïll. Others wore European clothes. Short bright coloured dresses with full skirts. To country girls like us they looked rich and sophisticated. Then I saw one with faint blue tattoos like mine, barely hidden by the skin-coloured powder on her face.

'Excuse me?'

I was relieved that we spoke the same language. She looked at us with pity. Poor country girls.

'We are looking for somewhere to stay. There are three of us, and we have a baby.'

She laughed a little, bobbing her head as if counting, adding the baby to the count with a different small gesture, her face despairing at the stupidity of girls fresh from the hills.

'Oh yes. So I see.' She moved back into her doorway, and sat on a high narrow step, taking a fresh cigarette from a pocket while she thought.

'I think Rose has a room. She's a fair woman to work for too. You could do worse. You see the door there, with the grill at the top. That is Rose's.'

We started to turn away, and she called after us.

'Can't you go back home? There's still time to go home. You would be happier in the mountains.'

My mother stood taller, and replied, 'We have no one left. The French took everything and everyone.'

The woman nodded and spat on the floor. 'Fucking French.'

The door was pulled open before we touched it, and we were confronted by a small woman who stared at us suspiciously. She looked first at the baby, then stared for a moment at our faces before opening the door wider, pulling my mother's arm as she brought us into the house.

'They'll be here soon. Best stay out of their way until we've sorted things out.'

She took us to the back of the house where a filthy kitchen backed onto a small courtyard. She grabbed our little goat and sent it bleating into the sunshine.

She started with my mother, taking off her scarf, and scrutinising her face. 'You're a bit old to start this, you know. But you've got a good body. There will always be someone who will pay, but you won't get much.'

Rose turned to me next, and pulled off my scarf, looking at me. 'You're younger and might do alright.'

My mother interrupted, 'She's just had a baby. She's still bleeding.'

Hayat and I looked at my mother, surprised that she would lie, and surprised that she would talk about bleeding to a stranger.

Finally Rose turned to Hayat. She looked at her thoughtfully. 'Have you done this before?'

Hayat nodded. 'I was taken for the Bordel Mobile de Campagne near Bou Saâda.'

Rose straightened up and looked at Hayat with a strange kind of respect in her eyes. 'If you've been a *whore there you can be a whore anywhere. You've worked your apprenticeship in hell. We'll look after you here.'*

My mother and Hayat had realised where we were, but it took me longer. We had walked willingly into a street of whorehouses.

Rose was a woman who was exceptional in the bedroom but best kept out of the kitchen. She had done all the cooking before we arrived at her bordello, making tasteless stews with rice and black-rimmed flatbreads. The food emerged from the crusted cooking pots into dirty bowls and the girls in the house took them, grateful not to be starving, but eating them without pleasure. Maybe it was because Rose's thoughts wandered, but when a client came into the house with one of our girls Rose would turn away from cooking to chat to the customer until the dark pungent smoke that accompanied her cooking began to fill the air. My mother took this advantage like a dying man offered water and negotiated with Rose. Rose agreed that if my mother did all the cooking, we could sleep on the kitchen floor, while Hayat worked in one of the rooms above. So that is how we earned our keep and Hayat earned the coins that make life more bearable, and buys a pretty scarf, or a lipstick or a new cover for the bed.

When we lived with the Tuareg I had learnt to cook to please my foster mother, but my cooking was nothing compared to the rich creamy stews, spiced zviti and chakhchoukha produced by my mother. We would go to the souk each morning, while Hayat and the girls slept, and haggle for pieces of lamb and fresh vegetables. We bought chillies for the zviti and spent hours cooking and chopping and pounding to make the dinners that the girls remembered from their childhoods. My mother made me learn each recipe, slapping my hands when I burnt something. Or if I didn't meet her expectations, she would look at me with despair.

'Oh Fatima, you don't dance. You can't cook. Be careful my girl, or you will find yourself working with Hayat!'

I understood why we lived as we did, but at the same time I felt sorry for Hayat. We had started as friends, but I realised that I came first, and I was protected. At the same time my mother felt guilty and would save Hayat the best little bites of meat and would find sweet pastries for when she came into the kitchen to chat with us while we washed her clothes. We cleaned the rooms upstairs, opening the windows wide to get rid of the heavy smell of warm male bodies that clung to everything including Hayat herself. She never complained. She had nothing and no one and maybe she was afraid that if she complained she would lose us as well.

Hayat would sleep all morning, and at noon she would put on a French skirt and shoes with little heels. She would brush her hair, and pile it on top of her head, applying face powder and lipstick before going to stand in the street next to our doorway, smoking with the other girls. She normally found a customer quickly because she was young and pretty and no one noticed that her eyes were dead when they were looking at her slim legs and firm breasts. And she was accommodating. The other girls said that she would do anything for money, even taking two customers at once, or trying to persuade the other girls to go into the room with her at the same time. I would sit outside the room with my ear pressed against the door trying to understand the moaning noises that came from the men and how they could sound as if they were in pain while in that room but leave with wide smiles on their faces.

My mother and I shared the small kitchen and knew better than to talk too much, or complain or fight or make a fuss, but I longed for the winds and fresh air of the Hautes Plaines.

The sunlight only found our courtyard for a few hours a day and 'as a woman who had recently given birth', I was allowed to lie cuddling the baby in the corner of the kitchen. Rose would come in from the kitchen and look at me, holding the baby in my arms, tucked against my skin.

'Are you going to cuddle that baby forever, Fatima?' she would ask.

'This house carries no one. Everybody works here.'

My mother stepped forward. 'She nearly died giving birth to Aïcha. She hasn't healed properly and is still bleeding. She is no use to any man. Leave her be with her baby for she will never have another.'

Rose looked at the cheapest cook and best cleaner she had ever had and decided to wait.

It was a month later that there was a commotion at the front of the house. A man was asking for Hayat. He was dirty and his breath smelt of alcohol. His words slurred together as he asked for my cousin.

'I want Hayat. She does all the things I like. I don't want anyone else. If she's screwing with someone else stop her and bring her here.'

Rose held out her hands, trying to calm him. 'She's working. Maybe you could see someone else today.'

The man looked behind at the girls standing in the street outside the bordello, and at the two girls sitting with their legs curled up on the couch. Then he saw me holding the tray of dirty cups that I had collected to take back to my mother in the kitchen and staggered towards me. 'What about this one?'

Rose stepped between us, but not before I saw the curiosity in her face. 'She has a new baby. She isn't working yet.'

The man pushed Rose to one side, before pulling down my apron. Putting his hand over my breast he squeezed hard. 'Is she making milk? I love a whore with milk.'

He started to undo the buttons of my blouse. I couldn't move my hands, unsure if I was more terrified of breaking Rose's cups or of what the drunk intended. He tore off the last two buttons before reaching forward to cover my bare breasts in his thick sweaty hands, pinching at them. I could smell the alcohol on his breath and tried to twist away, but he only pushed me closer to the wall, squeezing me more tightly. Rose pulled the tray from between us, still watching, as he put his mouth to my breast, mauling at me as I struggled to escape. Over his shoulder I could see Rose, watching and doing nothing to help me. Not knowing what else to do I screamed for Hayat and gave the high ululating cry that I had last heard at the caves.

I was rewarded by shouting coming from above, and Hayat rushed down the stairs covering her naked body in a pink nylon wrap as she ran. Seeing what was *happening she grabbed at the man's shoulders. 'Henri, what are you doing? I thought you only cared for me. You bastard!'*

Dropping the wrap so that it fell apart she slapped his back hard. He turned to look at her and forgetting me, his face lit at the sight of the half-naked young woman. Suddenly he pushed me away, full of apologies to Hayat. She smiled, gracious and forgiving, and told him to wait. A few minutes after she had run back up the stairs a French soldier came down looking flushed and furious, tucking his shirt into his trousers and doing up the buttons as he left.

'Rose, if you think I am fucking paying for her you're wrong,' he said.

Rose shrugged and watched him leave, before giving Henri a drink and pushing him towards the stairs.

'Up you go, Cherie. She is waiting for you now.'

When everyone else had left she turned to look at me. 'Go back to the kitchen, idiot girl. You could have made good money from him, but you're more useful cooking than screaming at the customers and upsetting everyone. Tant pis.'

Hayat kept none of her wages for the next month, but my mother was calm and happy knowing that we had a roof over our heads and enough to eat.

The baby flourished in that kitchen in our house of women and smiling readily was my whole heart.

One evening before the baby was weaned, just before sunrise and after the last customer had left, Hayat came down and sat with us, taking the baby to cuddle on her lap. She looked at my mother, and asked, 'Why does everyone think that all the Naïlli girls are whores?'

My mother shrugged and thought carefully before replying.

'It is the French that think it. When they first came to Algiers, they saw the dancing girls from our tribe and assumed that because they danced naked and had patrons, they could all be bought. They didn't realise that we only take a patron if we choose. That's why we all have the word prostitute on our identity cards. That's why they took you from Bou Saâda. Because they thought we were all born to be whores.'

'What if I don't want to be a whore?'

'Nothing changes in a day. Do you remember dancing with Jamila? I could teach you to dance, but you would need someone to dance with. Then maybe you could dance in one of the bars.'

I sat up straighter, and pretending a sacrifice I didn't feel, I carefully made the suggestion, 'She would need someone to dance with, a sister-dancer. I could dance with her. I remember all the dances and you could teach us.'

My mother looked at me, 'You're no dancer, Fatima.'

I looked back at my mother. 'Nor am I a whore. If we dance, we might meet husbands and get away from here. We can take you with us, go somewhere better. Maybe we could go back to the mountains . . .'

Hayat smiled a little smile, holding Aïcha close, rubbing the baby's soft hair under her chin. 'If I could find a man and leave here, I could have a baby like this, and never have to sleep with a man who doesn't love me ever again. I could find someone to take me away from here, and I would sleep all night, and wake in the morning to go to buy food from my family in the souk, like a proper woman.'

We said nothing more, each dreaming our own dreams, pretending it was possible, and that the next night wouldn't bring its trade.

By the time the baby could toddle my mother had taught us to dance and taking some silver she bought us the blue-white scarves of a Naïlli dancer, and silver coins to wear on our headdresses and round our necks. She told Rose that we were going to be dancers and said that Hayat and I would give her half our wages every day. Rose was a businesswoman and knew that two dancers could earn more than one whore. She sent us out into the night with her blessing.

We had arranged to join some dancers in a licensed café near the bordello. Two of their dancers had left to take their dowries back to the mountains, and the dancers that remained were older women. They needed new girls and accepted us happily. In the mornings they would spend time with me, trying to teach me how to move my hands elegantly and showing me the step-half-step movements of their feet. It is possible to be proficient at a thing while demonstrating no natural gift and that is how I danced. I knew how to dance, each step, each gesture. I looked like a Naïlliyat and dressed like one, but it was dancing with Hayat that saved me. She danced as if she was grateful for the music, and the freedom, and she carried me with her into a place far away from that street and its whorehouses. When they saw Hayat dancing the men would stop chewing their tobacco or smoking their cigarettes. They would gaze at our hands, twisting high above our heads, holding those beautiful scarves. Within three weeks my mother took our money and was able to rent a small apartment for our odd little family on the Route de Ranvier, and we moved away from the Rue des Ouled Naïlls.

When life is good it is easy to forget that nothing lasts.

Each afternoon Hayat and I would leave my mother caring for the baby during her nap and go to the European quarter. My mother didn't know that as soon as we left the Casbah we would go to a café and change into pretty cotton dresses, pulling on stockings and neat French shoes with kitten heels. We would wrap up our respectable long dark dresses in the wicker baskets we carried and pay a street vendor near the post office to look after them for the afternoon. She would shake her head and frown at us but pocket our money happily enough. Then we were free. We undid our plaits and wore our hair in tidy chignons and would walk along the waterfront, watching the fishermen repairing their nets. We would go to a favourite café and drink strawberry frappés and lemonade before suddenly realising the lateness of the hour and run back to the street vendor to collect our basket and return to dance.

It was the end of the summer when our lives changed once again. Hayat and I were popular dancers and had become aware that some of the men who came to watch were frequent customers. We were a little disturbed to see French soldiers in our audience, remembering Jamila's only night as a dancing girl; but as the weeks passed, we had found them generous and friendly. Hayat would finish our dance and kissing me on both cheeks whisper that she would be late, and then I would watch her putting out her hand and leaving with one of the men. I never went with them. I was thought of as a widow with a child to support and was comfortable with that. In my experience men had little to recommend them. They brought trouble with them, and the men in Jamila's life had destroyed her, and no one reminded me of Abdulkader.

There's a tap on the door. Two taps. Pause. Two taps. It's Grandmother, but she doesn't hurry into the room as she normally does. She's hesitant.

'Can I come and share the stories, Rabia? I've a story to add.'

So I nod, but I'm confused. I thought I knew all the stories. Grandmother comes into the room and sits on the wooden stool next to the table. She sits twisting her hands into her apron, waiting for me to finish mine.

After Hayat left, I would sit for a while with the other dancers, drinking sweet tea and watching the singers accompanied by the Naïlli drummers and musicians. It wasn't far to go home but Algiers was unsettled. The rebels were causing trouble in the European quarter, and increasingly gaining influence in the Casbah. We had quietly been advised to stay in the café after dark, so instead of going home I began to settle on the thick lamb's wool mattresses in the warmth of the kitchen, and I would lie in the dark, waiting for Hayat to creep in through the small door that led from the terraces. Kicking off her shoes she would crawl under my covers and hug me while we listened to the singing in the next room. One of the singers was my distant cousin,

Mohammed from the Hautes Plaines. He would sing traditional songs from the mountains as he tidied the café, and I would lie half-asleep listening to him. In the morning he would smile and come to speak to me, pressing his hands together in front of his chest in greeting. 'Did my songs please you, Fatima?'

I would smile and nod.

'Anything that reminds me of the mountains pleases me.'

I was only fifteen, and it was hard to believe that I was a girl who was mother to a small child, had lived for a year in a brothel kitchen, and now danced each night with the word prostitute on my ID card. Mohammed was much older. Maybe ten years my senior, and I didn't realise that he was singing for me. That was probably a good thing, because I wasn't looking for a husband, and had I been I would have appeared differently to him. It wasn't long before he started to follow me into the kitchen and sit with me in the little courtyard. He would look at me with his head tilted to the side as if there was something about me that he didn't understand.

'Were you married for long before your husband died?' His eyes were kind as he asked, and I hesitated, caught half between the desire for truth and the need for secrecy.

'My husband didn't die.'

Mohammed had been leaning across the table, looking at me, his hand a few centimetres from mine. He pushed himself onto the back legs of his chair, balancing. He looked disappointed. And worse, he looked disappointed in me.

'He didn't die, because there was no husband.' It

really wasn't helping. I had turned myself from a respectable widow to an unmarried mother in two sentences. I told him the truth because I was tired of lying.

'My baby . . . she's not mine. My sister died giving birth, and her husband was killed by the French on the same day. My mother told me to take the baby as mine.'

Mohammed's mouth had dropped open. 'Did Rose know any of this?'

'No.'

'So you lived at Rose's Bordello as an innocent, and stayed that way by pretending to be a mother and . . .' Mohammed's astonishment had turned to amusement. 'You must be quite an actress.' He sat, his large chest rumbling with laughter that shuddered through him as he wiped tears from his face. Then suddenly he sobered himself, and reached forward across the table, taking my hand. 'And you hate the French?'

I nodded. Unwilling to explain the things I had heard and seen the day that Jamila and Abdulkader died I raised my chin, and replied, 'I hate the French.'

Mohammed hated the French with a fury and passion that consumed him. He hated the way the soldiers walked the streets of Algiers as if they belonged there. He despised their women with their short skirts and bare arms. He saw the men drinking in the café where he worked, reaching out to the dancers as if they had the right to take anything that they wanted. They were everything that he despised, but I didn't realise how much until after we were married, and Mohammed had moved into the flat on the Route de Ranvier with us.

He was a man who never told anyone that Aïcha

wasn't my daughter, explaining that when we make ourselves vulnerable through lies, we must be careful to stick to the stories that we tell. I would like to think that he was an honest man, who was merely secretive, but I found out, when he died under the blade of a guillotine seven years later, that he was a consummate liar. But to this family he was a good man and a good father. We had no children together, Mohammed and I, but Aïcha was the daughter of our hearts, and I never felt a need to marry again.

CHAPTER NINETEEN

Fatima's story is over. I stroke my fingers across the words on the page. Amal sits up and takes the cahier from me. She looks at the three languages recording the story. I'm proud of my cahiers. Maybe, inshallah, I'll be able to tell the story to a daughter of my own one day. Grandmother moves the stool, scraping the floor.

'Do you want to tell us your story now, Mani?' Amal asks.

Mani sighs. 'It's only right that I tell you. I've told this story in my head so many times that it should be easier, but it isn't. I've told this story to two other people, but my only witness was Fatima, for the rest are dead. The last time I told this story it broke my family and broke my heart; but you have come to find out who you are Amal, and if I don't tell you important things will be forgotten, and I owe it to her that I tell you and Rabia the truth.'

'Her?'

Amal's question is ignored.

Fatima's husband was a strict man. He hadn't been brought up in the tribes, where women are free and own property and choose husbands and make the important decisions concerning themselves without a man to help them. Fatima and Hayat had grown up first with the Ouled Naïll with their oddly shocking independence, and then Fatima had gone with the Tuareg.

Did you know that when a Tuareg couple divorce it is the woman who keeps all their property, their tent and herds? The men get to keep their camels. Mohammed used to say that that was ridiculous, but I found it amusing that the men who had courted their wives, leaving their obedient camels grazing outside the Tuareg tents, would ultimately only leave with the camel they came on.

Mohammed was a good man, you understand, in his way. I remember him. He sang constantly. Traditional songs, and little funny rhymes. He would hug me and laugh at my pretend terror if he threw me up in the air, pretending he was going to drop me. I adored him, but he stopped Fatima and Hayat's dancing. He said that now that Fatima was married, she could be a good woman and that their dancing was over. He left the bar and found work as a mechanic in the city.

We stayed home, Mani Zohra, Amti Fatima, Amti Hayat and I. I loved Amti Hayat. She was a very quiet and gentle woman, but she had seen the very worst of men, and Amti Fatima told me later that Hayat was uncomfortable living in a small apartment under the protection of a man she wasn't related to. Her independence had been gained at great cost, and she became restless. Until Amti Fatima married Mohammed, Hayat had the freedom and forgetting of her dancing. She had the quiet evenings spent with men following the dance that led to the places she wanted them to lead. When Fatima stopped dancing Hayat had no sister-dancer, and she stopped dancing too; but without her dancing she became restless. She didn't have enough to think about, and we would come back from the souk to find her sitting at the little square table in the kitchen with nothing in her hands, staring at the wall. It frightened my grandmother, who would try to busy her, and put the zviti bowl in her hands, and give her things to do. I think that is why I always keep you girls busy in the kitchen. I don't want you to be like Hayat. She was full of sorrow and never told her story to us because it was too dreadful to share. Nothing is too dreadful that it shouldn't be shared; it is just that sometimes you only need to share with one person, or today with two of you. We, of this family, always tell our stories. We always share them, because then we can carry the weight of them together. But Hayat couldn't tell hers. Not to us. Maybe she was jealous because Fatima had found a little happiness, but I think she felt as if she had to leave, or she would feel lonely forever.

One day Amti Fatima came back from the souk, and Hayat had gone. Her dancing clothes and dresses had disappeared, but on the table, she had left her silver bracelets and her veil. I wonder about those bracelets, their design. I wonder if they started as slave bracelets, for dancers, but because our women were free, we added spikes to say that our bracelets weren't to defeat us, but to defend us. Her bracelets were like Jamila's.

Amti Fatima recognised them and told me that she had decorated them. She had wished happiness, and life and joy, and the bearing of children into the bracelets that she had helped to decorate. I think that is what Fatima found hardest. She had thought she had made magic bracelets that protected and blessed, but they hadn't protected Jamila and Hayat.

When Mohammed came home that evening he wasn't interested. He said to my mother that Hayat was a dancing girl and a whore, and it is hard to change a life. He said that we shouldn't look for her, because there would only be trouble for all of us if we did, and it was time for us to leave Hayat and the time at Rose's bordello behind us and live as respectable followers of the Prophet. Grandmother Zohra didn't seem to mind but I saw that Amti Fatima fretted over it for a long time.

When Mohammed was arrested, I know that Fatima wanted to go and find Hayat but remembering that Mohammed wanted her to be safe she said she would feel dishonest if she went looking. She said she owed obedience to the man who loved her. After he was guillotined in the prison courtyard for the murder of a policeman Fatima received a new respect in the Casbah, and the Arab quarter. She was a twenty-one-year-old woman, twice widowed by the French. She became a symbol of everything the Algerians hated about the French, and because of that she was never without the rent for her little flat, or food on the table. The men would see her in the street and pressing their hands together in front of their chests would acknowledge her, bowing their heads slightly. They did the same when they saw me. I was the daughter of Abdulkader of Bou Saâda, a Tuareg hero who had carried out a revenge attack for the rape of a twelve-year-old girl and tried to save a village from a massacre by luring the soldiers away. I was also the adopted daughter of Mohammed Kateb, who had been a martyr in the struggle for our country to be free. I loved who I was. I wanted to be brave too. I got my chance.

One evening a man came to our flat. He didn't introduce himself, but he told us that there was to be a war, and that the Algerians would, once and for all time, push the French and pieds-noir out of our country along with any Algerians who sympathised with the French. He told us that there would be a series of attacks, and that we would be safer moving into the Casbah. He moved us into this house. These rooms. It was one of the old Ottoman palaces, and it was a joy to be living in a large busy house full of women and children. I was fourteen years old. Within days the Al-thawra Al-Jazaa'iriyya had begun. The war for Algeria's independence. The war was fought in the streets and offices and cafés of Algiers, and went on for seven years, four months, two weeks and four days. Anyone with any intelligence understands that history is written by the winner of wars, but we must never forget that many people died who should not have died. It was a nasty, dirty, messy war with Algerians killing men who should have been their brothers, and the French torturing Algerians into false confessions and the betrayal of their own flesh and blood. I was fourteen when it started and could only watch.

There were bombs placed in the Casbah after the

curfew, and people who were doing nothing more than their jobs were shot on the street for being policemen or soldiers. At the time I believed I understood all of it. I thought it was a just war, and even the United Nations agreed that it was time for us to be free, but sometimes being free is just the beginning. Algeria still carries her scars, even though she tries to pretend that everything is well under her veil.

By the time I was twenty I was desperate to get involved, and everyone knew in our house in the Casbah that some of the men who came quietly across the terraces after dark were fighters. One evening I went up to the roof and waited. When the first man arrived, I stood and . . . well, it nearly ended badly. He had a gun and was jumpy and he very nearly shot me on the spot. When the next man arrived, he laughed at our horrified expressions and teased his friend, 'You can't shoot this one. She's the Tuareg's daughter from Bou Saâda.'

I was delighted that they knew who I was.

'Yes! And I am brave like him. I can fight like him and Mohammed Kateb!' I said.

The second man looked at me very seriously.

'You have forgotten that although they died bravely, they did die.' I was young, and when you are young you are indestructible . . . and I wanted to live in a country at peace.

'I know that,' I said.

They told me to go away and wait, and that a time would come for me to take my part in our country's fight. I wish I had been wiser. I wish I had understood then that when you have a country like Algeria its people must embrace their joint history. We are made of *many traditions, and there are many stories that should be remembered if we are to understand ourselves. You girls are both made up of the little parts of Algeria that we keep here and send away.*

Anyway, I'm avoiding my story. I should get on with it. I need to tell you and it might be a very long time before I have you both together with me again. As I said, my day came.

I was married by then, and Dahkman, my first child, was six months old. I left him with Mani Zohra when two of the women took me shopping in one of the large French stores. They bought me black patent leather shoes, stockings and lingerie, and a short-sleeved dress with flowers on it with a pale green cardigan. They bought me a patent leather handbag to match the shoes. A large bag. I thought I was so elegant. So cosmopolitan.

The same women had told me to stay out of the sun for weeks before the shopping trip. I told them I looked pale and ill, and they had smiled broadly, 'Yes, you do.'

I hadn't fully realised what they were doing until they brought me here, to this room, Rabia, and unplaited my hair. It had never been cut, and I wore the thin long plaits of a Tuareg but had plaited those together so that I could wear my hair like a girl from the Naïll Mountains. They didn't even bother to undo the plaits, they just cut them off. My hair was brushed, and shaped, and then they put makeup on my face, and lipstick, and I sat in front of that mirror bemused that I could look so French. I spent the afternoon practicing walking in the high heels, and then I was taken with two other women, to the old garage where Mohammed had been a mechanic. We were told what to do.

I was reluctant to hand them my beautiful bag, and I think at that moment I was more upset that I would lose something so real, not thinking about, not understanding what was to come later.

The three of us were told that we were to go through the checkpoint in and out of the Casbah, and that we had half an hour to get to our destination. Inside our bags were bombs. I don't know where the other girls went, and they don't know where I went. I went to a café near the Grand Post Office, and after drinking a lime frappé I tucked my bag out of sight behind a stool under the bar. That is the story that everyone knows. Brave Aïcha. Aïcha, who risked her life for her country. That's the story people know. But there was more . . .

I couldn't look at the other people in the café. I couldn't look around because I would have seen schoolgirls laughing over the names they had drawn in circled hearts on their notebooks, or maybe a couple falling in love over cups of thick hot chocolate. I might have seen the jukebox with the teenagers learning to jive to the bright music. I barely looked at the people sitting before I made to leave, but as I was about to reach the door I tripped, missing my balance in my new shoes, and was about to fall, when a man grabbed my arm, and helped me to steady myself. He was a man in his forties perhaps, a Frenchman. He asked me if I needed to sit down. He asked me if I was all right. I had about ten minutes left, but couldn't draw attention to myself by rushing out, so I said thank you, and sat for a moment. There was a woman at the table. She looked a bit Algerian, but like me she was dressed in a cotton summer dress with a cardigan tied across her shoulders. She looked familiar. And then I realised! I had found Amti Hayat! I was delighted. Overcome. I almost shouted at her, 'Hayat, it's me! It's Aïcha! Fatima's Aïcha!'

I could have forgotten my bag and sat and talked to her. There was so much I had to say. Instead, I pretended that I needed to speak to her alone.

She frowned.

'This is my husband, Étienne. You can talk in front of him. He knows everything about us.'

I pulled at her arm, 'I must talk to you. Please come outside.'

Hayat followed me, leaving her husband behind in the café. I had to talk to her. I had to get her away and keep talking to her. She was with a Frenchman. I couldn't explain to her what was happening. I would be arrested. I would be tortured. Other people would die. I had to do my job.

'Hayat. There is so much to tell you.'

'Well come back inside. I'll get you a frappé and we can talk for a while. I want you to meet my husband.'

'He seems nice. Are you happy?'

Hayat smiled at me. Her eyes were bright and lively, and her smile was wide. I had been five or six when Hayat left, and I had no memories of her as a happy woman, but here was a woman full of life and laughter. Time had healed her completely from the desperate years that she had lived through.

'Oh, I'm so happy Aïcha! We met two years ago, and we got married. Étienne will be here till next year and then we are moving to Paris. Imagine! Me in Paris! And

I have a son. He's in the nursery down the road.'

I was delighted. A reason to move her away from the café.

'Oh, how wonderful! You must take me there. Let's go now. I can't wait another minute to meet him!'

Hayat smiled, and said, 'I'd like that.'

Linking my arm through hers we began to walk down the road towards the nursery. I had done it. I had saved Hayat. My hands began to shake just a little, subtle enough for me to hide it. But then it happened. Hayat suddenly thought of her husband, with his kind grey eyes, waiting for her in the café, and pulling her arm from mine she thrust her bag at me, and ran back, calling over her shoulder, 'I'll just let him know where I'm going.'

Hayat ran inside, into the café, just as it exploded into glass and blood and body parts and burning death.

I was standing outside another café, and sat, dazed, on a small, round-seated, silver coloured chair. The chairs had curved backs, and a pattern of wrought iron leaves with thornless roses and hummingbirds sipping from hibiscus flowers. The chair legs curved outwards then, down into the clawed paws of a wild animal. I can still see the chair more clearly than anything else that day. I see that chair in my mind to stop myself remembering anything else. I sat on that chair for what seemed like forever.

A policeman came up to me, and asked if I was okay, and when I nodded rushed on towards the next person. A few minutes later another man came to me and asked if he could call anyone for me? Did I need collecting and taking home? Collecting and taking home. Oh no. I rose

to my feet, still holding Hayat's bag, and I walked
towards the nursery. Outside the nursery I took a deep
breath, then knocking on the door I went inside. The
women in the nursery were looking out of the window
at the police cars and the ambulances shrieking past.
They were ignoring the children. They barely registered
me when I said that I had come for Hayat's son. I looked
in the bag and saw Hayat's identity card. Sorry,
Madame Ancel's son. One of the women took a small
coat off a hook and grabbed a little lunch bag. The other
picked up a child and passed him to me. He squirmed,
trying to get back to the woman, but she pushed him
away and went back to the window. I picked him up,
wriggling and struggling against me, and carrying him
awkwardly against me I took him back to the Casbah.
What else could I have done? I knew Hayat had no-one.

Rabia and I are open-mouthed.

'But Mani, you didn't just steal a baby, did you?' I
ask.

Mani Aïcha shrugs. She is gathering the protective
shell back around herself as she does.

'What else could I do? He had no one. He was my
cousin.'

'He had his father.'

'His father was dead. I saw him lying dead with half
his face blown off. Hayat was dead too. I couldn't go
into the café and say that I knew Hayat. I couldn't get
involved. I just had to get home, but I wasn't going to
abandon that baby.'

Something comes to me. Suddenly I realise why
Grandmother is telling us this, why it is Amal and I

who need to know.

'Oh my God.'

Amal looks at me. Aïcha looks at me. Aïcha knows that I know, but I have to ask.

'Mani, who was the baby?'

Aïcha looks down and whispers, 'The baby was Mokhi.'

Amal and I look at each other. It's a stupid question but I have to ask, 'He was our dad though. We're still sisters?'

'Yes,' Grandmother replies. 'But–'

'You aren't our grandmother. Hayat was our grandmother.'

Grandmother looks tired. More tired than I have ever seen her.

'Yes.' She reaches into her apron pocket and takes out a little leather wallet. 'I have this.' She stretches out her hand and I take the wallet from her. The leather is old, and cracked along the spine, but inside there is a small glass frame, and a picture. Two young women, Naïlli dancers, with their arms wrapped round each other. Smiling. The woman on the left is Fatima. She has the same tattoos that I remember. Little squares and triangles on her cheeks and chin. Young and pretty. But it's not Fatima's face that draws me. It's the face of the girl standing next to her.

'Oh, my goodness. She looks just like us. Like me.'

I understand now, why Grandmother has hidden this photograph. Anyone seeing the image would wonder how we could look so much like this woman if she was just a cousin. Grandmother passes the wallet to Amal. She looks at the picture, and at me. 'Exactly like you, Rabia. Like both of you. I remember her every day. Each time I look at you. I can never get her out of my head.'

Am I angry, or shocked? I don't know how I feel.

'So who's Dahkman?'

'Dahkman's my son. Your cousin, not your uncle.'

This changes things. But Grandmother has been . . . Grandmother, all my life. And I get it. Why she didn't tell anyone. Dad would have been brought up in some god-awful French orphanage. Instead, he was in the heart of a family that loved him.

'Is that why Dad left? When you told him?'

Grandmother nods.

'He grew up hating the French and couldn't cope when he found out that he was French himself. He left. I thought he would come back, but it's been two years now. I don't think he'll come back now. I needed to tell you girls. I needed to give you back to Hayat. I can't change what I did. I'm not sorry for what I did. I was doing what I thought was right. What was best.'

'So that's why you taught Dad that we should never say sorry.' Mani nods.

'If you believe you're doing something with a clean heart there is nothing to be sorry for.'

'Are you sorry, Mani?' Amal asks.

'I have been sorry every day for fifty years.'

Mani picks up her bag, and leaves.

I sit with Mokhi's 'other girl', Hayat's other granddaughter.

'Does this change anything?' Amal asks.

'I don't think so. I'm still getting married tomorrow. It's all too late.'

I know why Grandmother can't bear to be with me. I know why she can't look at me. I also know that she can't make me marry Ali or anyone else. The rest I'll work on.

CHAPTER TWENTY

I was told to remember every minute of today. To savour everything and enjoy myself. But I don't want to remember. I want to wait to remember until it's real. Until there's someone waiting in the village church who wants to marry me for real. For ever. And I don't want it to be yet. I want there to be a day when I get dressed for someone else in my own time, instead of now, suiting everyone else.

We've been to the hammam. Me. Grandmother. Amal and Nassima. My other aunts, and some of the older cousins. I've been pummelled and prodded and bathed by the women. And they sang for me. I haven't been part of a bridal party at the hammam before, being unmarried, and I didn't expect the singing. They all know that this isn't my perfect day, and that Ali isn't the man of my dreams, but they still sang. As if it's real, to bless me.

I did know that I would be given the green gown to wear. It's old now. When Nassima got married she wore it. It is ancient, and the soft embroidery is fraying. They cover me in the gown and put towels on the floor. Grandmother is the oldest woman in our family, the Matriarch, and it is her job to apply the henna. She has been planning my henna and spent time looking at the little pictures I embroidered, including them in her designs. I have never seen ivy hennaed on a bride's feet, or bumble bees drawn taking nectar from a flower. I can see where Amal's talents came from. Except I can't see, can I? If Grandmother isn't ours.

We don't leave the house to go to a hairdresser, because I have chosen to be veiled, so Nassima can do my hair, and she brushes it smooth before fluffing it through her hands so that it curls round her fingers.

Nassima's dress could have been made for me. We are the same build and height. It's English. The dress has layers and layers of voile, and the waist is snug. As I suck in, I feel unable to breathe for a moment. Nassima smiles gently as she fluffs out my skirts. Weddings do that to women don't they? They remind you of the day that you were a princess. I have no problem being pampered, but all of this seems dishonest, especially when I see the expressions on the faces of the other women.

So I'll play this game. Be a puppet for the day. Lift my left arm. Grandmother paints the henna flowers. Painstakingly gently. It's the oldest lady in a family who paints them. Whether she's my grandmother or not she would still be the person with this duty. She leaves little ridged patterns on my hands. Then my feet. It tickles. Once the henna is dry, I pick at the thick brown lines before washing them off. Grandmother brings me a parcel wrapped in tissue paper, and hands it to me to unwrap. It's the veil that used to hang on my bedroom wall. I hadn't realised that it had gone. It's been washed, and smells of jasmine. It's the veil that Hayat wore when she danced. Nassima takes it from me and wraps it for me, as a scarf for my wedding, and rather than pinning it in place, anxious not to damage the fabric, Amal comes with a circle of jasmine flowers to wear like a crown on my head.

I go with Ali to register our marriage, looking for all the world like a bride. We say the legal words, sign the legal papers, and suddenly I'm Madame Bou Ibrahim, the baker's wife. Ali holds my hand tight, and no one stops us, even though it probably isn't quite the thing, and we go back to the Palace of Birds for our reception.

I go to my room to change out of Nassima's dress, and this time Amal brings me a dress that is the same blue as the sea in the bay when the sun shines, to wear for the religious words and blessing. I go downstairs, and the women start singing again when they see me. Uncle Dahkman gives me a hug, kisses me on both cheeks. Ali and I go stand in front of the Imam, and I'm married again. So many weddings for a girl who's getting divorced in a few months' time. Do they know looking at us? Do they know while they watch us cutting the cake? While we feed each other mouthfuls. They must know. After what happened outside in the street when Saïed died. They must all know.

I'm given my wedding ring. A lovely thing. Gold with small rubies decorating it. He slips it onto my finger and kisses my fingers as if it was given with love.

You know, the romantic kind, not the 'thank God you pulled me out of the shit' sort. At one point I think I see Khalid, but the flowers on my headdress make it difficult to see, and I'm not really sure. Over and over again my eyes are drawn to the fountain, which is running with fresh clear water that ripples over the patterned tiles. Then I know it is Khalid. He comes over. He smiles and puts out a hand that touches the ring on my finger, 'I'm sorry, Rabia.'

'Can I kiss the bride, Ali?' he asks.

Ali laughs, and leans forwards, 'You can kiss her in England if you come find us.'

Then there's that wonky smile, and Khalid rubs his fingers up through his hair. 'Ah, that's not fair.' He smiles over at Grandmother who is watching us. Completely focused on us.

'In England everyone kisses the bride,' Ali says.

I didn't know I could blush this pink. It is only after we've given out the cakes and sweets that we're allowed to go back to my room. The women have been busy, and there are fresh mattresses made into a double bed, with white sheets and red rose petals. There are candles burning, and the room is heavy with the scent of the flowers that fill the large jugs on the floor. Nassima has followed me up, 'Do you want me to help you get undressed?'

I give her a hug and stay there in her arms for a minute. 'We'll manage.'

Nassima shuts the door behind her.

'What do we do now?' Ali asks.

I laugh, and take my crown of flowers off, folding the veil carefully back into the tissue paper. I turn my back to Ali and lift up the back of my hair. He unfastens the long row of buttons. Then I make him turn his back before stepping out of the blue dress and hanging it on the curtain rail next to Bird. Then I go to my case and pull out some cotton pyjamas. Ali has been left nothing to wear and lies down on the bed in his wedding clothes. We lie together on the bed, and he wraps his arms around me. There is no curiosity. Not a kiss to be had. No passion.

'One day it will be your real wedding night, Rabi. But not tonight.' And that's fine. As it should be.

***

In the morning I'm awoken by Bird flapping against the sides of his cage. I go to the cage and put my finger through the little bars to stroke his breast, but he isn't interested and won't settle. Ali comes to stand beside me.

'What will you do with him? You can't bring him with us.'

I hadn't known, but suddenly it comes to me. I open the door of the little cage and spin the cage so that the door faces the sky outside the palace. Bird sits on his perch. He looks at me, his head on one side. Then he looks at the open door. It is only a moment before he is gone, flinging himself into the sky above our heads.

ACKNOWLEDGEMENTS

I would like to thank Louise Mullins and the team at Dark Edge Press for creating this book. Special thanks to Jamie Curtis for the cover design and Leanne Braithwaite for her editorial input. Thank you to Tony Millington, author of *Family First*, who introduced me to Dark Edge Press and suggested I contact them.

My first, much loved English teacher, Bill Horrocks, deserves many thanks for his encouragement and thorough grounding in the art of creative writing. He was the person who gave me the encouragement to dream of becoming a writer. This book wouldn't be complete if his name wasn't in these acknowledgements. I first met him, before he became my teacher, when my mother was preparing Bill's own manuscripts.

This novel wouldn't be what it is without the help of Martine McDonagh, my friend and tutor. Her critical input and advice helped me learn so much about myself as a writer and writing as a craft. Thank you to Mick Jackson for his ideas and insight, as he introduced me and the other students at West Dean to the writing life. I will also always appreciate the gentle intuitive wisdom and support from writer and poet, Mark Peter Howe.

I am grateful to the Algerian men and women that I met and spent time with for their affection, kindness and hospitality. This novel is my gift to them, and it is my hope that it will tell the stories that they shared with me. The stories I have discovered deserve to be told and are all based on things that have actually happened, although the historical details and dates have been altered and adapted with a significant dose of poetic license added in, in the hope that it does the stories of Fatima, Aïcha, Rabia and women like them justice, without causing offence. Please forgive me any mistakes or misinterpretations.

I am indebted to the women from Algeria who I found on social media, for their help in naming the characters in this story; helping me to give names that were appropriate to places and dates. Thank you for sending me photos of zviti, and the sticks that inspired me to give Mani Aïcha just such a zviti stick to wield against the crowd in the Casbah. You gave me the sort of information that no amount of more formal research could have yielded.

Thanks to my parents, Mavis and David Ridout, for their love and for teaching me and my sisters that little girls really can achieve anything they want to, so long as they work hard. And to my sister, Heather, for reminding me that it's never too late to become what we might have been. It is good to dream.

Thank you to Jo James, for reading all my novels and helping me to uncover the errors that hide in plain sight.

Thank you to my son, Sam. He helped me develop ideas and storylines over countless cups of coffee in cafés and coffee shops and during hours driving around Kent, with humour and good grace. Much of this novel has been written during days of 'table time', revising, studying and working together.

My last acknowledgement is my thanks to my husband Steve for his patience and support during the last thirty years of love and marriage. He always told me that I could do it, and that one day I would be published. Thank you, Steve, for believing in me.

Nicki has always had a passion for writing. Most of her writing takes place after midnight in the peace of her study when the house is quiet. In the summer she writes until the sky starts to brighten before sunrise. It's her favourite time of day and reminds her of happy mornings driving home after attending home births in Ashford and its surrounding villages, during her thirty-year career as a midwife. She spent years on night duty and has always been an owl when it comes to reading, writing and studying. Thankfully her husband has the patience of several saints, and her son has the same night owl tendencies.

This Place of Happiness was written as part of her Master's in Creative Writing and Publishing while studying at West Dean. Nicki is fascinated by the history of Algerian women and thinks that their stories are important and need telling.

Nicki lives with her husband and their four cats. Her husband and son both work from home which makes it a busy and happy place to be. She enjoys the long-term creativity of gardening, loving the optimism and expectancy of planting something and watching it grow. Much like novel writing. She also enjoys the meditative repetitiveness of needle crafts, painting watercolours and playing the flute and piano.

Love fiction as much as we do?

Sign up to our associate's program to be first in line to receive Advance Review Copies of our books, and to win stationery and signed, dedicated editions of our titles during our monthly competitions. Further details on our website: www.darkedgepress.co.uk

Follow @darkedgepress on Facebook, Twitter, and Instagram to stay updated on our latest releases.